The Temptation of Kate

by Peter Silsbee

BRADBURY PRESS
New York

Collier Macmillan Canada
Toronto
Maxwell Macmillan International Publishing Group
New York   Oxford   Singapore   Sydney

Other books by Peter Silsbee

THE BIG WAY OUT
LOVE AMONG THE HICCUPS

Bradbury Press
Macmillan Publishing Company
866 Third Avenue, New York, NY 10022

Collier Macmillan Canada, Inc.
1200 Eglinton Avenue East
Suite 200
Don Mills, Ontario M3C 3N1

Printed and bound in the United States of America

First Edition

10 9 8 7 6 5 4 3 2 1

Library of Congress Cataloging-in-Publication Data
Silsbee, Peter.
The temptation of Kate / by Peter Silsbee.—1st ed.
p. cm.
Summary: A demon fights for the soul of a young girl troubled by her parents' divorce and by a recent move from New York City to the country.
ISBN 0-02-782761-5
[1. Divorce—Fiction. 2. Moving, Household—Fiction.
3. Devil—Fiction.] I. Title.   PZ7.S5856Te 1990
[Fic]—dc20   90-1351 CIP AC

Thanks to . . .

Dick:
who gave me the idea
for this infernal book;

Barbara:
who wouldn't give up on it;

Dede:
who knows all about temptation;

and to C. S. Lewis,
for the kind introduction
to Beelzebub

1

In the beginning, Kate subtracted the easy things: the too-bright pizza parlor on Seventh Avenue that reeked of chlorine and sour lemons, the dank, dripping IRT subway platform at Grand Army Plaza where the homeless men slept on the benches during the winter, the newsstand corner where a barking black dog had bitten her hand on her fourth birthday—the places in her Brooklyn neighborhood she didn't like.

But when her mother began sorting out old clothes for the Salvation Army, holding stoop sales in front of their brownstone on weekends, Kate forced herself to go out to subtract the places she did like. She was a little surprised to discover that these were almost as easy to do as the not-so-pleasant places. Once she wrote them down in her sky blue spiral memo pad— Fountain − Fountain = 0, Bakery − Bakery = 0— the process, simple, abstract, and painless, took over.

It worked so well that she sometimes wondered what she would have done if she hadn't learned the trick. It was a lucky thing that the man in the library had shown it to her when he did, on the day her mother told her they were going to move from her nearly perfect life in New York City to an old farmhouse way up in the countryside near Canada.

But even so, after three weeks, she was not quite sure the subtractions would work on the really important places and people. She left the hardest, the special things for last, setting aside a page in her memo pad for each.

She began her last week on a Sunday, at the botanical gardens, subtracting the magnolia trees that smelled so mysterious and pungent in the spring; the green, cautious turtles in the Japanese pool; the rose garden where delicate blooms quivered in the soft summer breeze. All in all, it was easy.

On Monday in her room after dinner, under the heading of SCHOOL, she subtracted Dr. Kelly. Since school was over and she wouldn't have seen him until the fall, he was, in a way, gone already, and so he was easy, too. She subtracted the sunny, chalk-smelling classroom on the top floor, her classmates in descending order—from those she liked least down to those she liked best—then Dr. Kelly's cramped office stuffed with books and papers, the Styrofoam coffee cups on the windowsill, and the empty office down the hall where she and Dr. Kelly had played Ping-Pong for hours: she, chasing the scuffed and dented ball as it bounced weirdly on the linoleum while Dr. Kelly, standing on one leg like a bespectacled stork, whooped with laughter.

On Tuesday it got a little harder. She did Mrs. Ferguson, her old baby-sitter who lived across the street. When bent, old Mrs. Ferguson went to the kitchen to get ginger cookies and milk, Kate took out her notepad and subtracted all the souvenir ashtrays and Mrs. Ferguson's collection of sparkling ceramic poodles. When it came time to leave, Mrs. Ferguson gave her a kiss and told her not to be too sad about moving. But it was too late. Mrs. Ferguson was gone. On the way home, Kate decided people were harder to do than places or things. But not that much harder.

Wednesday was the day for the reflecting pool in Central Park. She took the IRT subway all the way up from Brooklyn, sat on her favorite bench by the Hans Christian Andersen statue, and watched children launch their little boats across the smooth, sunstreaked water. She too had once stood at the edge of the pool with her parents, pushing her white sailboat out into the pond. It had always been a bit like making a wish on a birthday, a magical, hopeful occasion.

On Thursday she visited Chuan Lee, her Taiwanese girlfriend, a quiet girl even shyer than she was who lived in a funny, wedge-shaped apartment overlooking Prospect Park. She asked Chuan to play her favorite Chopin sonata on the piano, the one that made her heart hurt. She found she barely felt a thing, just the memory of how the music used to make her feel. As she left, she reminded herself to subtract Jimmy, the redheaded doorman, too. Later, at home, she did.

But then came Friday. Greenwich Village. Six flights of worn marble stairs, the fishy, Friday-night smell on the fourth floor, the blasting TV on the fifth where the deaf lady lived with her dogs. On her father's apartment door there was a note saying he might be late, telling her to go inside and make a snack. She had been expecting the note—he was always late. She used her key.

Inside the deep, slanting apartment, there wasn't

much: his rolltop desk littered with unopened mail; the glass coffee table with his morning coffee cup sitting there in a dried ring; the scarred, white, vinyl foldaway couch; his books; the matching gold table lamps still sitting on the floor where he'd left them on the day he'd moved out of the house nearly a year before.

She lingered over a framed photograph on his desk, recalling the day it had been taken, a hot day in late summer at Prospect Park just after her eighth birthday. He was holding her over the water fountain, helping her get a drink, his long, already thinning hair sworled down over his forehead, his dark eyes filled with amusement and pride. She thought about taking the photograph with her. He was so young in the picture, not a single wrinkle on his lean, dreamy face. But she couldn't—she put it back down on the desk and subtracted the photo along with everything else.

He called around seven: at the office, couldn't get away, very sorry, asked her to come down and visit in a month. He said he would make it up to her then. She hung up, relieved. He would have been the hardest subtraction of all. She hadn't been really sure she could do it.

Finally came Saturday, moving day, and Kate only had to watch the subtractions as they were performed by the moving men. She stood in the bay window of the brownstone, arms tightly folded against her chest, watching the boxes, the tables, chairs, lamps, and rugs float down the front stoop on the movers' shoulders, watching all of it disappear into the dark maw of the moving van. As the high-ceilinged rooms began to echo around her, growing emptier and emptier, she grew emptier, too.

In the car, ready to go to their new house in the country, a house she had never seen, a house she had never even tried to imagine, her mother leaned forward over the steering wheel and twisted the bright knot of keys in the ignition. Then for Kate it all clicked into place: zero. She had finally made it. Finally reached that perfect, empty place she had been trying to get to for nearly a month.

Her mother touched her knee. "That's all right, Katie, you don't have to look if you don't want to."

Her mother didn't understand, of course. The house was already gone. Just like she was now. The final twist of the key had done it.

Subtraction. A simple, beautiful thing. Just like the man in the library had said.

2

MEMORANDUM

TO: His Most Malign Magnificence
FROM: Ballowe, Chairman, Disciplinary Review
RE: The Temptation of Kate Whitson

A transcript of my discussion with Demon 6166 in the matter of Katherine Whitson, of Black River, New York, will follow.

I shall await your recommendation. . . .

3

Surrounded by cardboard boxes, some with flaps flung open, some still taped shut, Kate and Ann Whitson sat on the floor in the front room of the Keener Homestead, their new home, a few days after the move. It was a warm evening, and the windows were open to the dewy night air.

"I still can't get over how quiet it gets here, can you, Katie? No fire engines or ambulances. No sirens. So quiet . . ."

Ann Whitson gave her daughter a long look, waiting

for a reply. When none came, she sighed, pulled a carton of books toward her, slit the taped seam with a paring knife, and glanced down at the spines.

"These are yours, too, Katie. Computer books. Katie?"

When there was still no answer, she spoke a little more sharply to her daughter: "Could you take them upstairs when you go to bed, please?"

Kate looked up from her book to her mother.

"What are you reading that's so interesting, anyway?" Ann Whitson asked.

"This book you gave me."

"Oh good—the tree one or the bird one?"

Kate glanced down at the illustration. "Trees."

Ann put down her paring knife, studying her daughter. "Katie, can I say something? You know, you've been very, very quiet since the move. Do you miss your friends? Do you miss New York? Can you tell me what's bothering you?"

"Nothing."

"Come on, Kate. Tell me what's wrong."

Kate knew she had to tell her mother something; she would just keep asking. Her mother was very stubborn that way.

"This isn't something that's wrong, but it's something I noticed. . . ." Kate began slowly. "Have you—I know this is going to . . . sound strange, but . . . have you noticed how, how—never mind . . ."

"What, Katie? What's strange? Tell me—"

"In the city," Kate began with more emphasis, having at last thought of something to say, "the sky is between buildings, at the end of the streets. Here in the country, it's all sky. . . . And it's all around you. And I don't know—it's kind of weird. But it feels like it's . . . I don't know—like it's pushing down on everything. I guess in the beginning it was just so different. . . ."

Ann tucked her chin onto her chest and cleared her throat. "Katie—be honest with me—and yourself. You're not happy. I can accept that. It's okay. You have a perfect right to be unhappy. I'm a little unhappy myself, you know. I'm unhappy at the circumstances that forced me, that forced us to make this move, angry at the way your father consistently failed to support—" She stopped, clearing her throat again. "But I accept my anger as a part of me. And I've learned to live with it. And I think you have to learn to live with it, too."

"I do."

"You *do* what? You do what, Katie?"

"I do."

"Are you being snide?"

"Snide? I don't—"

"I'm talking about *your* anger, Katie."

"But I'm not angry." You couldn't be angry at zero.

"Katie, Katie, Katie . . . Look—this move is a big step for us, emotionally, financially, intellectually. I want you to share it with me. Share in my elation, my fears, my frustrations. I want you to come out of your shell and *be here*. Don't crawl into your mathematical shell and pull the ladder in. Tell me what you're feeling. Okay?"

Kate nodded.

"Fine—now, aren't you just a little upset at me because I made the move up here?"

Kate folded her hands together. "I feel okay."

"Katie, all I want is for you to share your feelings with me for a change. That's all I'm asking. Remember before the . . . when you were little, how we used to talk?"

"I feel okay."

"That's it?"

Standing, Kate nudged a box of books with the toe of her sneaker. There was no sense in talking about her feelings if she didn't have any. "This box is mine?"

"And this one, too. Did you pack this, by the way?"

Kate glanced at the book in her mother's hand. "What is it?"

"Your father's Bible."

"No."

Ann tossed it into the box with Kate's computer books. "Well, anyway, take it upstairs when you—"

"See you in the morning."

"In the morning? Is this good-night?"

Ann watched Kate leave the living room, her slight shoulders bowed inward, staggering slightly with the weight of her books. As always, there was something vaguely prehistoric about her daughter, something unfinished and weirdly delicate at once.

"All right, Katie, good-night," she called. "And remember—I'm not all that happy either! So we can talk about it anytime you want!"

4

He came to the Keener Homestead about a week later, whistling a low, tuneless song between his teeth, walking through the shade of the stout oaks which grew a leafy canopy over Keener Road, casting his glance from side to side at the parched fields spiked with stubble.

Stopping at the big country mailbox, he noted the name "Whitson" taped across the front. From there, he glanced boldly around the property, at the scum-coated cattle pond that lay alongside the road and the gray barn on the hill behind. His gaze came to rest on the white frame house, its two distinctive black chimneys anchoring each end like garden stakes.

He reached down and scooped up a smooth, round pebble in his fingers. Spinning neatly on his toes, he slung it low across the side lawn. It struck the surface of the cattle pond with a flat, empty *plup.*

Stalking up the long dirt drive, he turned onto the curving flagstone path and mounted the broad steps onto the deep, old-fashioned porch. At the front door, he glanced into the diamond-shaped window and smiled at his reflection. Satisfied, he raised his fist and rapped on the door.

"Coming!" a cheery voice called from deep inside the house. "I'm coming!"

Upstairs in her room, Kate heard her mother's footfalls click briskly through the kitchen toward the front of the house. Putting her book down, she got up from her desk and walked quietly down the dim upstairs hall, curious. From the top of the stairs she watched her mother jerk open the heavy front door, saw the long shadow of their visitor fall into the entryway.

Though she knew it was not possible, for a sudden stabbing moment she thought it might be her father. Her father come to rescue her from this lonely, quiet, terrible place. The subtractions weren't working anymore. She had written a letter to her father telling him so, written it the night before, a letter which she hadn't yet dared to mail and maybe never would.

"Hi. I'm Nat Worthy," said a deep, smooth voice. "Thought I'd stop by and welcome you to the neighborhood."

"Hello, I'm Ann Whitson," her mother said in her nicest way. "Pleased to meet you, Mr. Worthy."

"Call me, Nat, please—after all, we're neighbors. And actually even colleagues in a way—I understand you're the new dean of admissions at State."

"Why yes—I am. . . ."

The man on the porch laughed. "I teach a couple of courses at the junior college—that's how I know— we academics are vicious gossips."

Laughing with him, Ann stepped out onto the porch, the screen door closing behind her with a gentle hiss.

"Sorry I haven't stopped by sooner. I've been away for a couple of weeks," the man went on. "But anyway, if you need any help with anything, you just let me know."

Kate wished she could see the visitor. He had a kind, soothing voice. She crept a few steps down the stairs.

"Thank you. Well, um, so, Nat—what do you teach?"

"Math. And speaking of math, I hear that you have a daughter, and that she's something of a prodigy. Her name is . . . Katherine?"

"Kate."

"I'm looking forward to meeting her."

"Today she's a little under the weather, a touch of the flu, I think. She—it was rather extraordinary—she fainted yesterday. She's never fainted before, and it was a bit frightening. But she's up, I heard her knocking around up there earlier. Let me call her. I know she'll be happy to—"

"Oh—that's all right. I can meet her some other time if she's indisposed."

A moment later Kate heard the creak of the rocking chair and the deeper, grinding note of the porch swing. They were sitting together.

She quietly descended the staircase and stole into the living room. There, through the sheer, white curtains, she saw the back of her mother's head and beyond, blurred by the milky drapes, their visitor's face in silhouette.

"So I understand from the grapevine that you and your daughter are from New York."

"Yes. Well, Brooklyn actually. But still insane, crazy New York."

Kate kneeled on the arm of the couch and looked through the curtains. A tangled ruff of hair, a high, wide forehead, a wispy beard: Handsome, she decided. He wore a stylish brick-colored sport coat and gray slacks. His arms were flung out and resting on the back of the porch swing, perfectly at ease.

"I'm not sure we're any more sane here in the country—there's just fewer of us."

"Are you from this area originally?"

"Oh no—I'm a Rochester boy myself. But I lived in New York during my college years." Good-naturedly, he embarked on his life story. After college, he told her, he had worked for a large public utility in the Midwest. But after the nuclear accident at Three Mile Island, he quit. "Nuclear power is inhumanly, inconceivably dangerous," he assured her. He moved to Black River, bought an old hunting cabin just down the road, cleared an acre of land, and took the part-time teaching job at the junior college to support himself.

"A back-to-nature sort of thing. So you're an idealist, then."

He laughed. "I suppose I am. Does that bother you?"

"Oh no, not at all. I think idealism is a fine thing."

Kate leaned closer. She found herself liking this man. His laugh, the way he wasn't afraid to say what he was thinking, the calm assurance in his voice.

"Don't get me wrong. I mean—I used to be very idealistic. That's why I got into teaching."

"When do you start work?"

"Tomorrow."

"Do you miss New York yet?"

"I haven't missed New York at all."

"And your daughter?"

"She's—she's coping. She realizes that it's better for us to live here in a less, well, in a more positive environment. I don't think she's thrilled, but these things take time."

"It can be tough on kids."

"Katie's handling it. She can be immature at times . . . oversensitive, that kind of thing. And like most gifted kids, she's a bit stunted in her emotional development. Not interested in boys yet. But I'm hoping that will change. Adolescence always rears its ugly head eventually."

A red stain of embarrassment crept up Kate's cheeks. Be quiet, Mom, she begged silently. He doesn't care about that.

"For the last three years she's been going to a special

advanced school at Columbia University, which, quite frankly, I felt, didn't help her much to mature," her mother said, lowering her voice into a more confidential register. "Kate's peers were deficient in social skills—like many gifted children. I want her to be exposed to real kids. That's one of the primary reasons we moved. She's at the point in her development where that's extremely critical."

"Growing up—I don't know how anybody lives through it."

Please, Mom, Kate begged. Talk about something else now. Stop talking about us. Stop talking about me.

"Now that she's nearly thirteen I want her to deal with the world on its own terms. She can't hide in her mathematical world forever."

Kate shifted uncomfortably on the couch. She couldn't believe it—her mother was making her sound like a math geek. Did she always do that with people, Kate wondered suddenly. Her insides shrank into a hard nut of shame and embarrassment.

She couldn't stand it. It wasn't fair. Standing, she took a deep breath, walked into the vestibule, wavered for a moment, but then stepped onto the porch, a little surprised at her own sudden nerve.

"Why—this must be Kate now," Nat Worthy

remarked, getting to his feet as she came out. He gave her an easy, inviting smile. For an instant, peculiarly, she thought she recognized him.

"Katie—this is Nat Worthy. Nat lives right down the road from us. He's a mathematician."

"Here, Kate—why don't you come sit next to me here on the swing," he offered, smoothing his hand over the cushion.

Kate gave him a nice smile and settled onto the porch swing beside him, feeling as she did so as if she'd won a small victory over her mother.

"I hear you're a math whiz, Kate," he said kindly, leaning toward her. "Tell me—are you interested in cusp catastrophes at all? I do a little consulting work on the side, and cusps are all the rage now in business."

"What kind of cusp?" she asked politely.

"Butterflies?"

"We were doing them a little . . . before school ended."

His eyes sparkled with interest. They were nice eyes, she decided, blue and quick.

"Oh really? You see I was hoping you—now the other, more selfish reason for my visit comes out—I was hoping you might be able to help me." He reached inside his jacket and drew out a manila envelope. "If you wouldn't mind, that is. . . . I've got my calculations here and if you could take a look. . . ."

"Well, isn't this great," Ann said, a little too enthusiastically. "Isn't this great, Katie?"

Kate slid her finger under the flap, curious to see his calculations. She hoped he was good, not just a number cruncher.

"Oh—don't look at it now," he protested, joking. "I didn't mean to come over and put you to work. . . . And besides . . . I've got to get going." He stood, smiling sheepishly. "I'm teaching a summer course. So I must take my leave. Nice to meet you both."

Exchanging handshakes with Ann, he turned to Kate. "Do you think I could stop by in a couple of days, Kate, after you've had a chance to look at that?"

Kate smiled and said he could. And when he left, walking back down the driveway, his shoulders straight and strong, she pulled out his calculations, scanned them, and saw that they were very, very good.

"Well—it looks like you've made a friend, Katie," her mother observed brightly. "And a mathematician. How nice for you!"

5

BALLOWE:	Gentledemons, our first candidate today is Demon Jaster—Demon 6166, singled out for his special new strategy in the case of one Katherine Whitson, the subtraction strategy.
	Welcome, Jaster.
JASTER:	Thank you. I am honored to be here. But I—
BALLOWE:	As you know, the Field Commendation Committee convenes every month to consider and reward those demons

who show true excellence in the field—the too-often-overlooked tempters of individual souls who are the very heart and soul of Hell.

As I've already told some of the board members, Brother Jaster, when I read of your subtraction strategy in your June report, I was very intrigued. And now I want very much to hear more about it.

JASTER: Yes, thank you, sir. I am very proud to be here, as I said, but if you don't mind, would it be possible for you to tell me how long this is going to take? The girl was on the very brink of suicide when I received your summons, and I—

BALLOWE: Rest assured that we'll make this as short as we possibly can, Jaster. Besides, the girl told you she would wait until morning to commit the lovely deed, and so—

JASTER: So you know what she said to me. You're aware—

BALLOWE: Of course, Jaster, of course—there's plenty of time for us to review the case

	before we witness the fruit of your labors in the morning.
JASTER:	Oh well, that's fine then. I wasn't sure if you knew about the—
BALLOWE:	Of course we do, Jaster. That's part of the reason we called you down this evening. We too want to share in your triumph. But before we do, I think it would behoove us all to hear some of the background of the case. Set the stage, as it were. Let me give a brief summary to the board—if you don't mind.
JASTER:	Not at all. No, go right ahead. I'm pleased. Very pleased at the . . . recognition.
BALLOWE:	Demon Jaster was assigned to Katherine Whitson in June of this year. Her previous caseworker, Demon Torsk, had been given a promotion in late May, hence the new assignment. We have some biographical material that Jaster received from Torsk when he first took up this case. You should each find a copy there in front of you. Page two in your information packets.

	Jaster—could I prevail upon you to read Demon Torsk's summary?
JASTER:	Certainly. *Katherine Whitson. Female. Age twelve. Born August 25, 1977, to John and Ann Whitson, an only child.* *Description: Plain-faced, brown-haired. Wears corrective lenses. No remarkable features.* *Special attributes: Talented with numbers. Attends special advanced math program at Columbia University.* *General Disposition: Passive. Complacent. No conception of good and evil. No known vices. Disinterested in boys, clothes, social intrigues, dancing, movies, etc.*
BALLOWE:	Thank you, Jaster. Good. Now, shall we jump right in? Jaster, why don't you begin by telling us briefly of the events that led up to your subtraction theory. That would be June third, your third day on the case.
JASTER:	Actually, if you don't mind, I think it would make more sense to start on June second.
BALLOWE:	Whatever makes the most sense . . .

JASTER: On June second, Ann Whitson, the girl's mother, got a phone call from the president at Black River State College. She was informed she'd been given the job of dean of admissions, a position she'd applied for some six months before.

BALLOWE: I'd like to read from your report of that week: *Ann Whitson wants to return to the place of her happy, carefree student days*. According to your notes, you felt the mother, Ann, was entirely selfish in her decision to pull up stakes and move.

JASTER: Yes. Oh, absolutely. A completely self-centered person, the mother. A career-ist.

BALLOWE: How did the girl react to the announcement?

JASTER: Passively. Later, in Black River after I gained her confidence, she told me that she was too stunned to speak. Her mother told her they were moving—boom—she froze—that was it. When I saw that, I knew I would have a very good chance with the girl. If I may elaborate?

BALLOWE: By all means—that's why we called you down.

JASTER: I would like to stress that the girl was not only passive, but had always avoided strong emotion. The only painful thing she'd ever had to endure was the divorce of her parents. In reviewing the case before I took it on, I thought my predecessor, Torsk, might have been a little lax during the divorce: He didn't exploit the ill will and bad feelings of the situation, preferring to let the girl slip back into complacency. That was his decision. And one with which I quite frankly disagreed.

BALLOWE: Noted. Now tell us about the genesis of the subtraction strategy. Was it a flash of insight, or had you thought of it beforehand?

JASTER: A little of both. Since she loved mathematics, I had thought about using this love against her. I wasn't sure how until I saw her wandering around the library.

BALLOWE: Tell us about that. . . .

JASTER: The day after her mother dropped the

bombshell on her, she went to the library to return some overdue books—also, I would guess, to get out of the house. She began to wander around the reading rooms, distracted, without purpose, or at least it seemed so to me.

BALLOWE: Let me interject here—wasn't it always difficult for you to determine the girl's mental state?

JASTER: I've had many who were much worse, much worse.

BALLOWE: How many?

JASTER: I would say a goodly number.

BALLOWE: You've been in the field for how many years now, Jaster? I've forgotten.

JASTER: Fifteen.

BALLOWE: And your predecessor in this case . . . let me see, ah yes, here it is—Torsk: 525 years. But back to the story—you were in the library, I believe?

JASTER: Yes. Anyway, after a while there in the library, I became convinced that she was beginning to sense the gravity of her mother's announcement. On an emotional level. She was in the children's area. There was a storytelling

28
≈

session going on, children sitting in a circle. I saw she was crying. Trouble. To show emotion in a public place. Dangerous.

BALLOWE: Tell the board why you thought that was dangerous.

JASTER: Well, as you know, any break in the day-to-day lives of these people causes them to think about larger issues. They take stock of their lives, tap into deeper wellsprings of emotion. And that is dangerous.

BALLOWE: Very good. I believe you were quoting from the Doctrine of Denial for a moment, weren't you? Very commendable.

JASTER: I try.

BALLOWE: Good—then came your brilliant idea.

JASTER: Yes, I knew I had to do something. I walked toward the girl, smiling, looking as sympathetic as I could. I sauntered over and asked if something was wrong. She grew flustered—she was, after all, a shy girl—she said there was nothing wrong. "When there's something wrong in my life, I just subtract

29
≈

it," I told her. Improvising, I took a call slip and a pencil from the top of a card catalog. "I can see you're sad about something," I said, "so let's subtract that." On the slip I wrote: "Sadness − Sadness = 0" and showed it to her. She looked at it for a very long time. "Is it the library that's making you sad?" I asked. "A little," she admitted. I took another slip of paper, wrote "Library − Library = 0", and gave it to her. "There," I said, "now there's nothing to be sad about, is there?" I left her staring at the equations, telling her she could use the trick on anything. "Subtraction," I told her, "is a simple, beautiful thing."

BALLOWE: I'd like to read a paragraph from your report of that week if I may. Here's what you wrote: *To my way of thinking we must encourage "subtraction" in every quadrant, the world over. As life becomes more intolerable, as the numbers of the wretched increase, as the environment collapses, we'll con-*

vince our subjects that the only smart choice is to deny, to forget, to subtract.

Pretty powerful stuff, Jaster. We don't often get such grand ideas from field operatives.

JASTER: I don't want to be a field operative forever, sir.

BALLOWE: So you're ambitious—good. As long as it serves our Master. But let's continue. The girl and her mother moved to the country. . . .

JASTER: Into a farmhouse about two miles from the nearest neighbor. Very isolated. A perfect place for me to begin my work in earnest. You see, I had decided by then that I would try something a little unorthodox. Not just nibble around the edges as I had been, but really take . . . um . . .

BALLOWE: Take a big bite?

JASTER: Yes, thank you. A big bite, exactly. I'd been reading a lot of our glorious history, poring over some of the great early temptations, and I thought I might try an older method—direct

	intervention. Insinuate myself into the girl's thoughts, introduce negative ideas, offer double-edged choices.
BALLOWE:	Contracts drawn in blood?
JASTER:	(Laughs) I wasn't going to go quite *that* far!
BALLOWE:	For the benefit of the board, I'd like to read from your report of their first week in their new house. *In this subtraction phase, she is experiencing everything on a coldly intellectual level.*
JASTER:	The girl was in a stupor, a trance. Except for the occasional odd moment, she barely spoke, never smiled—she was like some automaton: helping her mother unpack, lining up her shoes in neat rows, washing the floors. I thought she might be getting back at her mother by being supercompliant. But of course, she was only hurting herself. Which I was pleased to see.
BALLOWE:	But then, there was a small incident. Something happened, something you took as a sign of trouble.

JASTER:	The fainting episode? Is that what you're referring to?
BALLOWE:	Exactly.
JASTER:	I did not see the fainting as a sign of trouble. It merely meant it was time to step in and intervene on behalf of our Master.
BALLOWE:	Sorry . . . Didn't mean to put words in your mouth, Jaster. Go on.
JASTER:	Yes . . . well . . . about two weeks after they moved into that old farmhouse in Black River, Kate fainted. She had never fainted before in her life. Now, in my view, her emotions, denied and repressed for almost a month and a half, were reasserting themselves. Later that evening, I confirmed that when I observed her alone upstairs in her room—
BALLOWE:	You took the form of a fly, I believe?
JASTER:	Yes—why?
BALLOWE:	I just wanted to clarify that for the board.
JASTER:	I wanted to try some of the old methods, as I said.

BALLOWE: Go on.

JASTER: She stayed up half the night, writing a letter to her father. In that letter she told him she was not happy, that she was lonely, that she had no one to talk to. But she didn't mail it: She was uncomfortable with her feelings. She wrote another letter. A letter saying she liked the country, the quiet, the peace— all nonsense, all lies. That was the letter she sent. Very gratifying.

BALLOWE: Yes. Quite. Still denying her feelings. Very good.

JASTER: She was still trapped in the role of dutiful daughter. Trying to live up to her mother's expectations of how a mature young girl should act. And her father's, too, for that matter.

BALLOWE: And so you decided on your next bit of unorthodoxy.

JASTER: Yes. When I saw her faint, when I saw her write that first letter, I knew it was time. Time to bring forth a bitter shoot, nurture the black flower—as we used to say in the old days when we were more   poetic ... less ... well,   never mind. ....

BALLOWE: But what of your subtraction strategy?

JASTER: What of it?

BALLOWE: Why didn't you encourage more subtractions?

JASTER: I had moved on to the second phase, "subtraction by addition."

BALLOWE: Here, I confess, is where you lose me, Jaster. In your notes you say the same thing. How can you subtract by adding?

JASTER: By insinuating myself into her life before she could remember who she was.

BALLOWE: And so you paid the girl and her mother a visit.

JASTER: The first of many—a little unorthodox, as you say, but in my view, we must try a fresh, new approach once in a while. To keep sharp. And it worked: I did succeed, and it did get me noticed. After all, you did call me down. ....

BALLOWE: Indeed we did. Now, let's continue. I read from your report of that week: *Whenever I can, I turn our conversa-*

tions back toward her former life in New York. I stress over and over how perfect her life must have been there. I force her into the past, into wishing for what is gone, idealizing what went before. . . .

6

At the first faint hissing from the ridge road, Kate closed the book in her lap, sat up straight on the porch swing, and listened: There was a car coming. She hoped it was Nat Worthy. Nat Worthy in his dusty red pickup truck.

In the two short weeks she'd known him he'd already become a friend, in some ways an even closer one than her childhood friend Chuan Lee. Talking with him, doing math with him, helped her remember who she was, released her from the silence and emptiness that had so quickly become her life.

With her mother away at work most of the day the old farmhouse was a very lonely place. Every morning, waking, Kate squinted at the red numbers on her digital alarm clock, trying to squeeze out some reason to get out of bed. There was little to entice her; certainly the dark, silent rooms with their creaking floorboards did not. As often as not, she rose only because she hoped Nat might stop by to fill up the silence with his friendship, with the bright dance of numbers as they worked together on an equation.

But his visits were sometimes painful, too—he reminded her of what she had left behind in New York. He liked to talk about his student days at New York University, going to jazz clubs in Greenwich Village, in Harlem. He had even lived in Brooklyn for a year and knew exactly where she had lived, knew all about the Italian bakeries, the botanical gardens, and the library.

He always said exactly what he was thinking, and she liked him for that. Like the second time he came by he said: "You look miserable. It must be hard for you. To come here, to be plunked down in the middle of nowhere like this." And the next time he came, right in the middle of solving a problem he looked into her eyes, sighed, and with a slow shake of his head said: "I bet you miss your old classmates at Columbia. Too bad there was no way for you to stay in New York." She felt a dark, secret pleasure when he said things like that, true things she wouldn't dare to say out loud.

After one visit, she went up to her bedroom, took out the sky blue memo pad, and looked at all the people and places she'd subtracted before leaving, hoping to find it healing somehow, the way looking through an old photo album can be healing. Instead, it made her more lonely. Those things were gone forever. Like locked doors in a long hallway. She could only wander up and down, never could she go back inside. Nat was right when he said: *Too bad there was no way for you to stay in New York.*

And yet, at the same time she realized that if she'd stayed in New York, she'd never have met Nat Worthy. One day she'd told him so, saying, "Well, I miss New York a lot, but I never would have met you in New York." He'd smiled, thanked her for the compliment, then said: "But I'm sure you'd trade me for New York any day of the week. Be truthful now— let there always be truth between us." Blushing, she had agreed.

When she heard the hissing stop at the intersection

of Post and Keener roads, she knew then it wasn't Nat. Her heart sank in disappointment. In the month she had lived in the farmhouse this was one of the things she had learned—that a stop sign meant something for country people, even on an empty road. Nat never stopped; neither did her mother.

The growl of the approaching vehicle grew louder. As she waited to see who it would be, she decided that the next time Nat said something about how sad it was for her to have been uprooted from the city, she was going to tell him he was right. He would listen and understand. Not like her mother, who only pretended to and then lectured her on how good it was to live in the country.

As she watched, a dusty black and tan station wagon at last came poking over the crest of the hill, gathering speed as it came down. Soon the passengers became visible: A man wearing a black, wide-brimmed hat pulled down tight over his ears was driving. Beside him sat a woman wearing a big, straw hat and dark glasses.

As the car came closer, nearing the base of the drive, it slowed, then veered over the white line. Surprised, Kate watched the car nose past the big aluminum mailbox and roll up the gentle grade toward the house, small stones and gravel popping and spitting out beneath the tires.

Tall, thin, and starved looking, dressed in a black flapping suit, the man got out, an old man with deeply sunken eyes and strangely luminous skin. He walked around the back of the car and opened the passenger door. Reaching in, he helped the woman out. Standing slowly, majestically, the woman smoothed a hand over her plump stomach, then turned to the porch and shot Kate a penetrating, knowing look. Short and stumpy, dressed cheerfully in orange pants and a white print shirt, she took the man's arm and pushed herself erect on an aluminum cane. Together they walked across the lawn, ignoring the flagstone path, the pink rubber tip of her cane setting off soft explosions of dust as it struck the dry grass.

Just short of the porch, the woman gave Kate a taut, practiced smile and wished her a good afternoon in a loud, clipped voice.

"Hi . . . Um, if you're looking for my mother, she's still at the school," Kate answered.

The woman shook her head and leaned forward on her cane. "No, young lady. I came to talk to you," she said brusquely. "And do you know why? I have a gift. I can tell with just one look whether or not a person has accepted Jesus Christ as their savior. And I can tell—I could tell all the way from the road—that you have not."

Kate saw her visitors in a new light: Religious nuts—that's what her mother called them. Her mother always closed the door on religious nuts and, if they persisted, shouted at them to go away. Her father would almost always talk to them and sometimes, if he had his wallet, give them money.

"My name is Audrey Peel," the woman continued, "and this here is my brother Ezra. Ezra is a mute. I tell you that so you don't think he's got no manners."

The old man showed a row of ragged yellow teeth.

"I see you're reading a book there."

"Yes," Kate replied, staring down at the cover.

"What's your book about?"

"Um, trees . . . It's about trees. Their names and stuff."

Her mother had bought it for her—*The North American Tree Identification Handbook*—saying she should learn about "all the natural beauty around us." Dutifully, Kate was trying to read it, but mostly she spent long hours staring at the pictures and thinking about the flowers in the botanical gardens back in Brooklyn, flowers in neat and tidy rows, with their names on discreet black and white placards.

"I've got a book, too," Miss Peel said forthrightly. From underneath her arm she produced a black book with a gold cross embossed on its cover. "It's a book called the Bible," she said. "The Bible tells about the Tree of Life. And about the blessed who wash their robes so that they may have the right to the Tree of Life."

Beside her, the man called Ezra made a low rasping noise.

"And how the remnant of the trees of His forest will be so few that a child can write them down," Miss Peel intoned. "Have you heard about the end time, young lady, when the Lord shall make all things new?" Miss Peel stared at her. This time she seemed to want an answer to her question.

"Oh . . . no, um, well, like . . . when the universe collapses?" *Was that what she was talking about?*

"Listen, child—do you know that up in Heaven you won't have to wear those glasses," Miss Peel said, touching the frames of her own. "No more scratching them up or losing them or seeing the eye doctor. Won't that be nice? I know myself that I can hardly wait to get rid of these old glasses of mine. Won't that be a blessing?"

Kate sat back on the porch swing, considering this. "I've always worn glasses," she admitted after a moment.

"Well, you won't have to wear them in Heaven," Miss Peel went on. "And no contact lenses neither. Your eyes will be bathed in heavenly light. And night shall be no more; for the Lord God will be their light, and they shall reign forever in Heaven. You know about Heaven, don't you?"

"Well, I don't go to church . . . uh . . . so I don't really know much about it, but doesn't a person have to . . . have to, um, die to get to Heaven?"

"Have you ever been to church?"

"Well, a few times, but, so I don't . . . but . . . um . . ."

"What's your name?" Miss Peel asked.

Kate told Miss Peel her full name: Katherine Whitson, the way she always did when introducing herself to an adult.

"Katherine—if you believe, you shall have life everlasting. Have you ever read the Bible, Katherine?"

"No."

"Goodness, Katherine, in the Bible, Jesus says: 'Ye must be born again.' Did you know you could be born again this very instant? Ezra and me could do it for you. What do you think of that, Katherine?"

"Is this like the Tree of Life you were talking about before?"

"Pardon me, Katherine?"

Katherine, Katherine, Katherine. Kate didn't like the way Miss Peel kept saying her name. In her mouth it sounded sharp and insistent, like a hammer striking every sentence home.

"Yes—like a hypothetical tree. I mean, once you're born, you're born. You can't be born twice."

"Katherine," Miss Peel went on, "the man who used to live here, Joseph Keener, was a member of our church. We used to have baptisms in your pond over yonder. We had revival meetings in your barn. Preacher Shore saying the holy words, girls in white dresses, boys in their Sunday suits getting baptised in the Holy Spirit. You know, Katherine, unless you're born of water and the Spirit, you cannot enter the kingdom of God."

It sounded like a simple equation to Kate: if not A then not B.

Miss Peel paused for a moment, studying her. She quoted more scripture: " 'That which is born of the flesh is flesh and that which is born of the spirit is spirit.' "

A equals A. B equals B, Kate thought. She looked up at Miss Peel, blinking, trying to understand. "Does B represent um . . . Heaven?"

Ezra, his old hand shaking, held out an orange flier with a picture of an explosion on the front. Radiating from the center was all manner of debris—television sets, cars, buildings—flying off into space. Off to one side stood an angel with a sword.

"Is this um . . ." Kate wanted to be polite. "Is this supposed to be the universe collapsing—is that what this picture is?"

"That's right. And it's coming soon. Very soon," Miss Peel told her. "And only a small remnant shall remain."

"Well, not for a few million years," Kate disagreed. "And the sun is going to burn out a lot sooner than the universe is going to collapse. And nobody will live through that."

"You read that pamphlet and then come see us," Miss Peel suggested, though it sounded more like an order. "Our place is right down the road from you. By the four corners. And our church is just before the four corners. Come on Sunday, child."

"Um . . . well . . ."

"You read that first. Then we'll talk serious. Nice to meet you, Katherine. God be with you." As suddenly as they had come, they left, arm in arm across the lawn, folding themselves into the station wagon, backing down the drive, and heading away up the hill.

Kate took off her glasses, held the frames a few inches from her eyes, and squinted through the lenses. "That would be nice," she whispered. Heaven. Perfection. Just like her old life in New York.

7

Tucked into the back of a shallow dirt clearing about a mile from the Keener Homestead was the small, ramshackle church of Miss Peel's and Ezra's faith. It was a church like many another on the outskirts of small towns: founded by a vigorous young minister with a small and loyal congregation, prospering for a time, then gradually falling into disrepair and decay as shepherd and flock dwindle, grow old, and pass away.

Kate knew nothing of the history of the church. She only knew that she felt like she wanted to walk past it, and maybe—if Miss Peel was there—ask some questions about the orange pamphlet. Nat had said it was mostly mumbo jumbo and gobbledygook, but he did agree that it was interesting, especially when Kate pointed out the part about the big bang and how close it was to what the physicists said.

When, after a ten-minute walk in the hot noonday sun, Kate finally reached the church, she was disappointed: there was no one around. In fact, the church looked abandoned. She wondered if she'd come to the right place.

Walking over to a string of whitewashed boulders marking the boundary between the parking lot and the woods, she sat down on a smooth, domed rock in the sun, pulled out the pamphlet, and reread it, trying to make some sense of the strange words and ideas.

Reading the pamphlet for the first time on the porch, she had decided that it was written in some kind of code. She thought maybe the Tree of Life stood for something else, and the darkness and the light and the void were values which had symbolic meanings. Like in algebra. She thought maybe that was why people went to church, to learn the code. To learn that the darkness stood for negatively charged electrons, that maybe the void was a black hole connected to another universe. She wondered if God represented pure energy, the gigantic spark that touched the superdense mass to cause the explosion of Creation.

Her father had once said something like that. Physics could only explain what happened after the Creation, he'd said. It couldn't explain why. Kate had once stood with him on the street while he talked for nearly an hour with two nice ladies, fresh from church in their flowery dresses and white hats, about the Creation. Demurely, they assured him it was God who set the universe in motion. He kept asking how they were so positive. They said because the Bible said so.

Behind her a small cloud of black flies swirled out from the woods. She didn't notice them until they descended close to her face and frightened her. Abandoning the rock, she walked across the sunny lot into the shade, leaving the small swarm circling the place she had left.

She watched the insects, sunlight glistening on their tiny wings. They seemed to be tracing a kind of lopsided spiral. By reflex, she began thinking of ways to describe their behavior mathematically; but she hadn't come to think of numbers that morning. She had come to think of the Alpha and Omega, the beginning and the end.

The Bible had started at the beginning, her father's

Bible which she had been reading at night, so her mother wouldn't know: reading the Creation story, the spirit of God moving over the face of the waters, the waters bringing forth swarms of living creatures and also the great sea monsters.

There was a kind of binary operation underlying everything, she had decided: darkness and light, good and evil, death and life, water and dry land. But it was more complicated: the water and the tree also contained their opposites. Adam was put to sleep, and God made Eve out of one of his ribs. So Adam also was two things: a man, but a man who had once contained the beginnings of a woman.

As she read late into the night, it was with a peculiar combination of recognition, mystification, and disgust. She knew the stories of Adam and Eve and Cain and Abel, but reading them from the Bible was different. A flaming sword guarded the Tree of Life; Abel's blood called out to God from the ground. She had never thought the Bible would be so violent and terrible.

She had always equated God with peace, with infinity—numbers endlessly adding together, clicking one after another into a bright abyss. She imagined a white-bearded old man sitting at the end of the last number, smiling, benevolent, gathering all the bright numbers up into himself—not this God who rained blood and fire.

Her God knew everything, but in particular, he knew the workings of numbers. He knew about perfect numbers, for instance. And not only perfect numbers, but perfect theorems to explain why numbers behaved in their rational and irrational ways. Often, when she was solving a problem, she felt a kind of perfection flowing through her thoughts, felt the answer coming into existence as if it had always been there, that all she was doing was uncovering it, finding it like a jewel buried in the dust. It was as though God had placed it there.

She heard the rush of a car on Keener Road, heading in her direction. If it was Nat, she thought, she could talk to him about God and the void and Creation. They could talk about perfection. Like her father, he liked to talk about these things. In fact, the last time he'd come over they'd sat in the grass at the edge of the cattle pond and talked about the "interesting correlations" between the "life-giving water in the Bible" and the theory of the "cosmic soup." "It just goes to show you," Nat had said with a laugh, leaning back in the grass, "how scientists use the notion of special water in their own creation fictions."

But it wasn't Nat coming down the road; it was

her mother's blue Toyota. Disconcerted, Kate watched the car close in—her mother was supposed to be in school all day, just like every day, and to see her pulling into the church's small parking lot, waving, honking the horn, didn't make sense.

"Out for a little walk?" her mother called, rolling down the window, smiling. "It's a good day for a walk."

Kate went slowly over to the car. "What are you doing . . . um . . . I thought you were—"

"Would you like a ride home?" her mother interrupted cheerfully, reaching over and unlocking the passenger door. "I decided to come home and have lunch with you today."

Kate hesitated—she would have liked to stay near the church and think about God and numbers—but then she nodded and got into the air-conditioned car. The vinyl seat, cool beneath her thighs, made her shiver.

"Buckle your seatbelt—safety first—there we go, and lock the door." Her mother waited for her to perform these small tasks, then, smiling, said: "So I went to school, and since I was just about the only one there, I thought we could—Katie—where are your glasses?"

"Um . . . I . . . decided not to wear them today."

"You walked all the way down here without them? Weren't you afraid you'd walk into a tree?"

"My eyes aren't that bad," Kate said, responding seriously to her mother's teasing.

"Hmm . . . you know, you look much prettier without them. Much more, um, much less serious."

"I was thinking, in a perfect universe . . . I wouldn't have to wear glasses."

Ann smiled, patted her daughter on the knee. "In a perfect universe, you wouldn't have to wear anything. But since we don't live in a perfect universe— what about some contacts? I think you should be old enough for contacts now. Would you like that? An early birthday present."

Kate reproached herself for mentioning "the perfect universe." It was her secret. Her special secret with Nat. But the offer of contact lenses intrigued her. No glasses—like when she was a little girl, before her eyes went bad.

"Maybe that would be okay," she said after a moment.

"What's that you've got there?"

"What?"

"In your hand. What is that?"

Her mother studied the explosion on the cover.

"It's a . . . pamphlet."

"What kind of pamphlet? Let me see."

"It's about the collapse of the universe, I think," Kate explained quickly as her mother took the pamphlet. "It's in a kind of code, though. I don't really understand it yet."

Frowning, Ann opened the flier. "Where did you get this?"

"From a lady. Who stopped by. A few days ago."

"This is not about the big bang, Katie. This is about Armageddon."

"What's Armageddon? I saw that, but I didn't know. . . ."

"It's . . . well . . . it's sort of the Christian version of the end of the world," Ann explained. Handing back the pamphlet, she made a face, her eyebrows pinching together. "I really think you're too young to be worrying about religion, Katie. Way too young. I don't really approve."

"But . . . I'm not worrying about it, Mom. I just think it's interesting that they believe in the big bang. Like physicists. Nat thinks it's interesting, too," she finished weakly.

"I saw Nat today. He stopped by for a chat."

"But don't you think about it sometimes, Mom?" Kate continued.

"Think about what?"

"Don't you ever think about how the universe got started?"

Her mother shrugged. "It's not really an issue with me. Nor do I think it's an issue with most people. And frankly, I think your time would be much better spent . . . I'll see what I can do about finding someone, some kids for you to get to know. Maybe Nat knows some people. He must. Then you . . . can stop worrying about this . . . this stuff."

"I'm not worrying—I'm just thinking about it, that's all."

"Katie, I realize there's not a lot for you to do during the day, but it's up to you to make good use of your time. Why not go for walks—take along that tree book I bought you. If I didn't have to work, I'd be having the time of my life, learning the names of things, taking hikes."

"I *was* taking a walk."

"Look Katie—we talked about this before: I don't think you're adjusting to our new situation very well. And I'm concerned. When I try to talk to you, you're either distracted or off on some tangent. I want to know what you're feeling, what you're thinking about. That's not too much to ask is it?"

"No . . ."

"So? What are you feeling? Are you lonely? Angry? Sad? Do you miss the city?"

"Yes."

"Yes, what? Which one?"

"I miss the city."

"And why do you miss the city?"

"Because I'm not there."

"And you're sad about that."

"Well, but it's not like I'm sad, really. It's more like—do you ever think about Heaven?"

"The city was like Heaven—is that what you mean?"

"Back when you and Daddy were married it was."

Ann pointed at the pamphlet. "Is this what got you started on this 'Heaven' business?"

Kate shrugged.

Ann took the orange flier from her daughter's hand, popped open the glove compartment, and tucked it inside. "You know," she said, "you really do look much prettier without those glasses."

"Mom?"

"Yes, Katie?"

"Mom—I . . . I . . . There's nothing for me to do here," Kate said, the words spilling out. "You have work, but I don't have anything to do . . . I mean

57
≈

there's no reason for me to be here. I want to go back to New York."

Ann, surprised, recovered by speaking in her most teacherly way: "Of course there's a reason for you to be here, Katie. So you can be out of the city, meet some normal kids your own age. Grow up in a normal environment. We talked about this months ago and—"

"But Mom, when school starts, I'll come back," Kate interrupted, plunging on, making up a plan as she went along, feeling its rightness. "I'll stay with Dad just until school starts. I really miss the city and my friends and everything. All I want to do is stay with Daddy for a few weeks. Then I'll come back. Please."

"I don't think your father . . . I don't know how your father would feel about you showing up on his doorstep for two months. I mean let's be realistic about this."

"But if he said I could go, then could I go?"

"Why not go for walks . . . I tell you if I were you . . . or wait until you meet some people. I really—"

"Just for a few weeks—please?" Kate begged. "Please?"

The pleading note in her daughter's voice softened Ann's resolve. "I tell you what, Katie, I'll be very blunt with you. I think it's a bad idea ... but ... if you think ... we'll see how your father feels about it. And if it's okay with him, well, then we'll work from there."

"Really? Oh—Mom—thank you," Kate exclaimed, clapping her hands together in her sudden and unexpected joy.

"I'm not saying you can go, Kate, I'm just saying we'll think about it," Ann said crisply. "But in the meantime, I don't think you should be talking to these people. Once they get their hooks into you, they never let go. Like those two Jehovah's Witnesses your father invited in for tea—I finally had to scream at them to make them leave."

Kate wasn't listening to her mother's lecture. She was already imagining herself back in New York, taking the subway down to her father's neighborhood, flinging open the door to his apartment. She felt a deep stirring of pleasure, of hope, of anticipation.

"Thinking about God is all part of growing up, Katie. And sometimes growing up can be a painful thing. But it's all for the best. We learn, we grow, we figure things out, and ultimately we learn to take responsibility for our lives. Nobody else is going to do that for us."

Across the lot, the swarm of flies shimmered and rose above the trees.

8

BALLOWE: So you decided to "add" yourself into the girl's life.

JASTER: Yes—appeal to greed, envy, gluttony, sloth, an assortment of the old sins. She was greedy for company and I came. Greedy for a sympathetic ear—there I was. She envied her former life in New York; she was jealous of the girl, Kate, who used to live there. And gluttony—she developed a taste for my company. Sloth—she did not go out of her way to make other friends (not that I gave her much of a chance). Anger—everyday she was increasing her capacity for it—anger at her mother, anger at the course her life had taken.

BALLOWE: We get the idea, Jaster, now—

JASTER: What I'm saying is this: the old methods are all one of a piece, brilliant in a way. Do you see?

BALLOWE: I believe we do, yes. You're saying that you're a rather brilliant fellow.

JASTER: (Laughs) Well . . . no, not exactly. I'm saying the old methods are brilliant.

BALLOWE: Where were we?

JASTER: I was telling you about adding myself into the girl's life.

BALLOWE: Go on then . . .

JASTER: What I did was, I got her fixed on the idea of perfection. Everytime we solved a new problem, I would exclaim over and over the beauty of numbers: how problems had solutions, how they were perfect constructs, perfect numbers, that sort of thing. Closed perfect worlds. Tidy answers. I would let her escape into an equation, then drag her back out with some observation about how imperfect her life was in Black River.

That really upset her; I enjoyed that—I was really quite good at it, you see. And she developed quite the little crush on me. And why not? I was charming, interested in her, talked to her—she couldn't help herself.

BALLOWE: But then you encountered a problem: the girl was visited by a pair of fanatics.

JASTER: The fanatics weren't a *problem*. Not at all. If anything, they were a help. You see—

BALLOWE: I read from your report of that week. *Fanatics have contacted Katie. Idea of Heaven seems to fascinate her. Asked mother if she could go stay with father until end of summer. Mother is considering it. This could be a problem.* Those are your words, Jaster.

JASTER: Well, I wrote that in the heat of battle, of course, before I had a chance to think. When I had collected my thoughts, I saw the whole fanatic thing as compatible with what I was doing. I had her thinking of perfection. They had her thinking about Heaven. Heaven as New York and her father: the same thing that I had been doing: getting Kate to think of her former life as a kind of ideal construct. They were reinforcing me; we were acting in concert. Kate began to think of New York as Heaven, Heaven on earth.

We even had a few theological discussions. At which I'm very adept, if I do say so myself.

BALLOWE: *Girl thinks of nothing but going to New York. Mother stalling, afraid of being too lenient.*

She must not go. Kate must fester, must blame her mother, must actively hate her life here.

And here, Jaster, you stepped in again. This time with the mother.

JASTER: I'm very proud of this bit of business. Very proud. I went to visit the mother at the college. Dropped in, bringing doughnuts and coffee. I made some studiously offhand remark about Kate to start the conversation and *boom*, that opened the floodgates.

Ann Whitson told me all about Kate's desire to go to the city and stay with her father, how she couldn't make up her mind one way or the other. And I listened—I'm rather good at pretending to listen—and I um-hmmed and uh-huhed and bided my time as she prattled on, waiting for her to ask me my opinion. Finally, she did.

In reply, I told her a bogus anecdote—one which I made up on the spot. "Well, Ann," I said, "last semester I had a student who got very homesick. A freshman, a girl, very shy—a lot like Kate, actually—and she got into the habit of going home every weekend. Which meant she never got into the swing of things socially. By the time Christmas rolled around, she had decided to drop out. I didn't think it was healthy for the girl to run home—I mean it can be tough in the beginning, but if she had stuck it out, made a few friends, she'd probably still be in school."

"That's what I've been thinking," Ann said, brightening up nicely. She was relieved, of course, to have someone confirm her thinking. "In the long run," she said, "I think it will be better for Katie if she stays."

"Yes, I think so," I agreed. "But don't tell Kate I told you so. I couldn't take the responsibility of disappointing her like you poor parents do."

I tell you, I walked out of that office positively burning with excitement. How easy it was to manipulate the woman! Much easier than Kate. Kate was always so tentative, difficult to read. Even last night in the parking lot, I got the—what time is it up there now? Are we—

BALLOWE: We've plenty of time. Four hours until dawn. Please continue.

JASTER: It's just that I'm so excited. You understand. Now, where was I? Oh, yes. Later that evening, Ann went home and told Kate the story about the homesick girl and used it as the basis for saying Kate couldn't go to New York. When I saw how terribly disappointed and upset Kate became, I was positively on fire!

The next day I went over to "commiserate" and found Kate in a truly delicious state of depression. She was so low, so miserable, so defeated that she began to confide in me, really confide in me for the very first time!

BALLOWE: And you reaped "an unexpected benefit" according to your notes. . . .

JASTER: Yes, yes! She confessed that she'd had another reason for wanting to see her father: to see if she could somehow, some way, get her parents back together. Their divorce had shaken her to the core. She was wounded by it and in many ways blamed herself for the split. "I didn't do enough to make them stop fighting," she told me. "I should've made them talk to each other and stop being so angry." She told me that one of the bones of contention between her mother and father had been the question of her education: Her mother wanted her to go to a regular school; her father wanted Columbia. As she confided more and more in me, I saw how very hard she could be on herself. I was very, very happy to see this. It meant she had a deep capacity for self-destruction. And so, naturally, I began to formulate new plans.

As we talked, I got her to really think about how perfect, how "heavenly" it would be if her parents *did* reunite. And over the next few days, I got her to think about ways this goal might be achieved. "This cancelled trip is only a battle in a larger conflict," I told her, "getting your parents back together. That's the real goal here."

Of course, getting her parents back together was an altogether impossible fantasy. Even more doomed than going back to live in New York. Doomed fantasies lead to broken dreams, do they not? Broken dreams lead to despair. And despair, if nurtured properly, gives way to thoughts of revenge. And in the weak and unworldly and sheltered, thoughts of revenge can lead to thoughts of self-destruction. Subtraction, if you will.

I schemed and schemed, trying to think of some impossible, futile, dreadful way she could reunite her parents. And eventually I came up with a kind of object lesson for her, a true damned-if-you-do, damned-if-you-don't dilemma. I get a thrill of malice thinking of it even now!

BALLOWE: The trip to the waterfall?

JASTER: Yes, the waterfall . . . exactly!

9

"I'm afraid the falls aren't much to look at this time of year," Nat apologized, leading the way down the stony bank. "But in the spring with the melting snow from the Adirondacks, the view can be quite spectacular."

With an expansive smile, Nat stepped up onto a boulder beside the nearly dry streambed. He gestured at a rock outcropping, pointing out a smooth, elbow-shaped indentation worn into its face. "See there— you can see how high the water gets, and how fast it roars through here. The falls are only a trickle now, but in the spring, you can hear the falls all the way back to the road."

Kate could easily imagine both the falls and the roaring river. All along the streambed there had been signs of the strong current: the polished boulders lining the banks, big tree limbs lodged between rocks. Standing on the riverbank overlooking the falls, she saw thousands of sparkling pebbles covering the basin floor some forty feet below—like some huge gleaming carpet—where the phantom river had deposited them before rushing off downstream.

They stood at the edge of the streambed, listening to the furtive trickle of the summer stream, Nat pointing out interesting rock formations, the small pools of trapped and stagnant water, his voice as smooth as the boulder he stood on.

Daddy would really like this, Kate thought. Whenever they went to Prospect Park in Brooklyn, her father always gravitated to the green, humpbacked bridge at the south end of the park. There, he would lose himself in the dark, turbid water rushing underneath . . . back when she was little and life was perfect.

"It would be nice if there was a footbridge."

Nat looked back over his shoulder: "What?"

"Oh . . . nothing . . . I was just thinking. . . ." She had spoken her thoughts aloud without realizing it, something she had begun to do recently with Nat. The first time it had happened, a few days before, she had been abashed at her lack of control, but now, she began almost to revel in her lack of restraint and in the small dangers of it.

"Thinking about New York?" he asked, smiling. "How did I know that? Was it your wistful expression? Tell me, Kate, have you come up with any plan to . . . to get things back on track yet?" he asked. "To solve your problem? Get back your life?"

She looked down pensively at the trickling stream, pleased by Nat's penetration of her mood. "Well," she began softly, "the only thing I can think of is calling my dad and telling him I *have* to see him . . . but . . . he . . . he always—if my mother says I can't, he won't. . . . But I can talk to him. He'll listen. Not like my mother. He misses when we lived in Brooklyn, too. . . ."

"Kate, the problem with being your age," Nat summarized, "is that you have no power. No way to influence things. No leverage. When your parents were divorced, your father could move out: power. Your mother—able to pull up stakes and leave New York when she wanted: power. But you, *you* have no money, *you* can't get a new job. You're still their child. *You're* stuck. The only leverage you have is yourself.

I mean, you are worth something to your parents. Only if you were gone would they see how much you are worth to them."

"You mean like . . . like if I ran away?" Kate was a little surprised at Nat's suggestion: Adults, even adults who were friends, were not supposed to suggest such things. But then Nat was more than an adult friend. More than Dr. Kelly, even. "I did that," Kate confessed after a moment. "I went to Chuan Lee's for one night. But . . . it was stupid because my mother knew where I was. She came and got me in the morning."

"What you'd need is a place they'd never look. Or threaten something terrible, death and destruction," Nat joked. "That'll get their attention."

"I was thinking . . . maybe if I wrote him a letter and told him how I really feel about things. . . ."

"You're afraid he'll say no, aren't you?" Nat said seriously. "That's why you won't send that letter."

"I almost sent it," Kate protested.

"You've already written it then," Nat remarked.

"Yes, I did. A while ago."

"Kate, you need to find a way to fix it so they can't say no—that's what you need," Nat said. "But . . . I don't suppose there's any way to do that, is there? Aside from threatening death and destruction."

He was joking again, she thought, being light, trying to cheer her up. When she didn't answer, he lowered his voice and spoke seriously: "What you need is something foolproof. That's what you need. Something powerful."

"What?"

Nat gave her a small, sympathetic smile, cocked an eyebrow. "I daresay you've been thinking about it for weeks now, haven't you, Kate?" he said shrewdly.

He looked her straight in the eyes. In the split second before he'd spoken, Kate had experienced a moment of uncanny understanding: She'd known what he was going to say. Not the words exactly, but his thoughts. Nevertheless, she pleaded ignorance.

"I don't know what you mean. . . ."

"Don't deny it, Kate," he went on, the bantering note creeping back into his voice. "It's perfectly normal for someone your age, someone in your situation, to contemplate such a thing. I contemplate suicide myself when things aren't going my way. There's nothing wrong with it."

He jumped off the rock, came up beside her. "Am I right, Kate? You know it's okay to think about it. Believe me. And I'm going to say something that may shock you. I even think it's okay to do it. I'm a realist. You're a realist too, aren't you?"

"I . . . I try to be. . . ."

"Think of people in serious life-and-death situations, say someone in the desert with no hope of sustenance or rescue—isn't it more courageous and dignified to choose to end your life yourself, choosing the time and place, rather than having some outside force decide? Or consider someone who is to be put to death, a prisoner perhaps, who hangs himself. Isn't he more courageous and realistic than someone who dully waits for the switch to be thrown? Why hang on to life when it's not worth living? It's illogical. The solution is always in your hands."

"I guess . . . in certain situations . . . but . . ." Nat had surprised her with this little lecture. She didn't quite know what he was saying, even as she heard and understood the words.

"That's all right, Kate, we don't have to talk about it now if you don't want to," he said seriously. He smiled, consulted his watch. "Anyway, I've got to get back to town—errands to run." Touching her shoulder, he gave it a squeeze, a kind of tender signal that the conversation was at an end. Kate was grateful; he knew when she didn't want to talk about something, just like a true friend.

But Nat was right. She had been thinking about such things. Sitting in the house, alone, occasionally she would find herself wishing everything would just stop. Especially after her mother told her she couldn't visit her father. She would begin to wonder what it would be like to go beyond zero, fall completely off the axis, drift into the null set. It wasn't exactly that she thought of ending her life; no, it was more like she wished the sadness and emptiness and impotence would come to an end.

Quietly, she and Nat retraced their steps along the bank, cutting back into the fragrant woods, following the pine-needled path that led to the road and the dusty red pickup. In their mutual silence, Kate felt a new kind of closeness to Nat. He truly was someone whom she could tell her deepest, secret feelings, who would treat her with tenderness and restraint.

Nat stopped in the middle of the path, held up a hand. "Listen," he said softly. "Do you hear that?"

She did: a sort of ticking, scraping sound, very close.

Putting a finger to his lips, he crouched down and carefully lifted the lowest branch of a scrubby blue pine.

What she saw made her stomach drop. Laying on its side, panting furiously, was a gray squirrel spattered with blood, its hind leg caught in the jaws of a rusting metal trap.

Kate looked away, but it didn't help. She could still

see the squirrel in her mind, its bulging eyes filled with terror.

"You see any big rocks around here?"

"What?"

Nat let the branch fall, scanned the surrounding woods. "A nice big one. Ah—there's one."

"A rock?"

"To put the poor little guy out of his misery."

Kate stared at him. He was serious.

"His leg's obviously broken, Kate. If I let him go, he'll die a slow, painful death, probably starve."

She glanced down at the base of the pine tree, realizing what Nat's words meant. "But you can't . . . you can't just . . . there must be something else. . . ."

Nat pursed his lips thoughtfully, looked at Kate for a long moment, then asked, "What, then?"

"Well . . . I don't know . . . maybe we could take him to a doctor—"

"Kate—be realistic—his leg is crushed. He's a wild animal—he's not a house pet. You can't just take him to a vet and get him fixed up."

"Why not—I mean . . . they can put him in a cast or something and then—"

"They don't eat in captivity—he'd starve—he'd starve in a cage instead of in the woods. Same difference." Nat sighed. "I understand how you feel, but it's the kindest thing we can do, Kate. We've got an animal out here who's going to die no matter what. Now if you want him to starve, we can leave him. If you want me to leave him here so he can be someone else's dinner, we can do that, too. If you think about it rationally, you'll see that the only thing we *can* do is put him out of his misery. It will be over in a second and would end his suffering—you saw how he was suffering—he's got his leg half chewed-off as it is."

Kate closed her eyes, fighting back the sick feeling in her stomach.

"I'll do whatever you want me to do, Kate. If you want me to leave him here—then we'll do that, but I think you're being terribly cruel. Terribly cruel."

"But to kill him . . ."

"It's the kindest thing we can do, Kate. Believe me."

Kate closed her eyes tightly. It was too terrible to have to choose. Nat chose for her.

"Open your eyes, Kate, and hold up the branch," Nat said, his voice steady and serious beside her. "It'll be over in a second, I promise."

She felt his two strong hands on her shoulders, guiding her toward the rustling tree. The next thing she knew, she was holding the branch. Nat was bending down next to her, carefully poking a stick under the tree.

Risking a glance downward, she saw Nat using the stick to pull the trap out. Seeing a flash of blood and the quick, agonized thrash of the squirrel, she closed her eyes again, so tightly that tears stung at the corners.

"Just hold the branch," he said in the same steady voice. "You don't have to look. It'll be over in a second."

At her feet the squirrel made a series of furious chittering rasps. All she could do was wait; the scuttling and thrashing grew louder and louder until she felt as if she were going to scream. She sensed a sudden movement beside her, something brush against her arm.

In a kind of horrible blur, she saw Nat's arms coming down, his eyes charged with a wild gleam, and felt a queasy thump at her feet. Where the squirrel had been, now lay a smooth gray boulder nearly twice the size of her head.

"It's all over," Nat said calmly. "Come on—it's all over. We can go now."

"I need . . . okay . . . just a minute. . . ."

"Quick and painless," he said. "A simple, beautiful thing."

Kate blinked back her queasiness and looked up at Nat. Something was wrong. Something didn't make sense. "What did you say?"

"Quick and painless. Come on, let's go. I want to call the game warden about that trap. Those antiques are illegal."

"No—after that—the simple and beautiful thing . . ."

He cocked an eyebrow. "Well, it was . . . I mean, in a way."

"No, but . . . did you ever say that to me before?"

He shrugged. "I say a lot of things."

"But the man in the library . . . he said the same thing . . . simple, beautiful thing."

"What man in the library?"

"The man who told me about the subtractions."

"What are you talking about?"

Kate stepped back, stared at Nat, looking for something—she wasn't sure what. His eyes, deep and knowing, returned her gaze. He smiled, and as he did the strange feeling of recognition evaporated. And yet, even so, a trace of something else remained: a stirring of unease about her friend.

"Come on, Kate," Nat said, taking her by the elbow and nodding toward the path that led to the road. "Let's get going."

10

Late that afternoon Ann Whitson came home from work to tell Kate some important news: Her father wanted Kate to come to New York and she, Ann, was giving permission for a weekend visit. It was news Ann hoped would cheer her daughter. Kate, in Ann's opinion, had been unbearably withdrawn recently.

She swung her briefcase up onto the kitchen table with a loud *thunk* and walked briskly to the back staircase; she hadn't much time to talk to her daughter. "Katie! Are you here?" she called. "I have to go

81

right back out to a meeting soon so if you're up there—"

"Wait! Don't go! Mom—Help me!"

Kate appeared at the top of the stairs, her usually pale face suffused with emotion, her fearful eyes wide, hair disheveled, damp, and sticking to her cheeks.

Ann remained rooted on the bottom step for one long moment, staring at her daughter. She'd never seen her so utterly upset. *Distraught* was the word she thought of to describe her daughter's appearance. Recovering herself, she went quickly up the stairs, took her daughter by the arm, and walked her down to the kitchen table.

"Here—let me get you some water," she said busily, taking charge. "That's right—you just sit here for a minute and relax, then you can tell me what happened. Here now, Katie. Now, relax, take it easy. Take the water."

Kate drank the water, her hand shaking, then asked for more. Bringing the pitcher to the table, Ann sat down beside her and gently stroked Kate's arm. She was suddenly very frightened for her daughter.

"I don't have to leave for a few minutes, Katie. So just tell me when you're ready. Once you let it out and tell me, you'll feel better."

82
≈

Kate gathered herself together and managed a bleak smile.

"Are you okay now, Katie?"

"I took a nap . . . and I had this nightmare," she began slowly. "It was . . . I was sitting on the front porch, reading. Then the two . . . church people, the man and the woman, came driving right up onto the lawn. The people I got the pamphlet from. The ground was all wet and everywhere they stepped the grass turned black . . . black footprints. The woman came up onto the porch and started talking to me. And her brother did, too. In real life he couldn't talk, so I knew I was dreaming. And I looked and saw that the woman didn't have her cane. Or her glasses. But I still had mine."

Kate looked out the kitchen window at the side lawn, her face growing somber. "And I felt this burning inside my chest, this terrible burning. I thought I was dying. I really thought I was dying—"

"Maybe you've got a fever," Ann interrupted. "Let me feel your forehead. . . . You do feel a little warm to me."

"And the man, he reached over and touched my lips and said: 'Speak.' And my lips burned. The woman took off my glasses and told me to look over at the pond. And I could see it clearer than ever. Down to the bottom. And then it . . . and then the pond started to bubble up and overflow onto the lawn. The grass filled up, the water flooded up. I knew we were going to drown and I stood up and I told them: 'Look out! The water will burn you to death!' "

"That's terrible, Katie," Ann said, shaking her head. "No wonder you're so upset. Let's get you upstairs and—"

" 'The water will burn you clean, burn you to death!' "

"Katie—you're getting yourself all upset again."

"And the water rose until it covered me. And it burned. It burned so bad—"

"Settle down, Katie." Ann stood up, laid her hand on her daughter's thin neck. "You're going to make yourself even sicker this way."

"No! Listen! I—I was inside the water and it was black and thick and burning me. But the burning felt good, too, awful and good. I felt something terrible brush up against my leg. I knew it was terrible. I could feel how gigantic it was underneath me. Then the water—"

"Katie—did you drink a lot of soda this afternoon?"

"I died! I felt myself dying!"

"Answer my question, Katie. Did you drink a lot of soda this afternoon?"

"I knew what it was like to die!"

Ann stood. "Katie, I think you should go upstairs and lie down and take it easy. Let's get you back to bed, and let's make sure you make a stop at the bathroom. It sounds to me like you had a very full bladder—dreaming about all that water."

Kate looked down at her open hands, her eyes wide. "I know what it's like to die, Mom. I never knew before."

"You'll be fine, Katie, just fine. We'll get you some aspirin, and you'll be just fine after a little rest."

"It was terrible, but it was so terrible that it was . . . I don't know. . . . Because even though I was dying, I knew I had to die so that—it doesn't make any sense, I know, but—I had to die so I could do something. . . . I can't explain. . . ."

After leading her daughter upstairs, while Kate was in the bathroom, Ann went into her room and found the windows closed, the room hot and stuffy. "No wonder you're feverish!" Ann called down the hall. "It's like a furnace in here!"

After opening the window, she went to her daughter's bed and straightened the sheets. As she did, she discovered her ex-husband's Bible underneath the

85
≋

pillow, with the orange pamphlet tucked inside as a bookmark. She was still examining it when Kate, pale but composed, came into the bedroom.

"Have you been talking to those religious nuts again, Kate? You can tell me the truth, Katie."

"No . . . I haven't."

"Then why are you reading the Bible?"

"I'm not . . . reading the Bible."

"Don't lie to me, Katie."

"I'm not," Kate protested. "I was, but I'm not anymore."

"Then why is it under your pillow?"

"Because I . . . why are you looking there anyway?"

"Kate—I told you I don't think you should be reading this stuff."

"I'm not," Kate said sharply, a blush of color creeping up her neck.

"Well, if you say so, then I'll have to believe you," Ann said doubtfully. "Here, sit down here—I have something to tell you."

"What?"

"Sit down here for just a second."

"What?"

"I'll tell you what—it's about your father. I talked to him today on the phone and he—"

"What—is it something bad?"

"No, Katie, not at all," Ann said with a brisk smile. Now that the crisis had passed, she was concerned about getting back to her meeting. "He wants you to come down to see him next weekend and . . . I think . . . it would be a good idea if you went and saw him."

"He wants . . . what? You do?"

"He wants to see you. He's sending up a bus ticket. But just for the weekend."

How could it be possible? How did her father talk her mother into it? How had he known how badly she needed to see him? She'd never sent the letter.

"He's very busy. He's going on some trip. But he wants to see you before he goes. Anyway, I've got to get back for a meeting. So fix yourself a good dinner. See you around ten."

"But Mom—why are you letting me go?" Kate asked, following her mother to the door and out into the hall.

"Because your father wants to see you," Ann answered over her shoulder.

"But when I wanted to see him, why didn't you—"

"Because this is different, that's why," Ann replied, already halfway down the stairs. "I'm really late now, Kate. I'll see you later."

Kate turned and walked back to her room. She was going to see her father. It was too incredible; something she had so fervently hoped for to come about. All at once, she grew excited and began pacing up and back alongside the bed, but then just as suddenly stopped and sat down on the bed, overtaken with a peculiar feeling of shame and anger.

"I shouldn't have told her about the dream," she said aloud, looking down at her hands. "I shouldn't have told her." The dream had been too personal, too profound to share with anyone, not even her father. She shivered—the burning water—she could feel it yet.

But her father—she was going to see her father. She stood up, began pacing again. Now she could tell him how badly they needed to get back to their old life, their perfect life.

Walking out of her room, down the long hall toward the front staircase, she barely noticed where she was. What could she say to him? How could she convince him, make him see that they had to all live together again in New York?

Halfway down the front staircase, she stopped, clinging to the banister with both hands. "I will not think about that dream," she said, her voice dying in the dim stairwell. "I am not going to think about it again."

11

Nat leaned back into the porch swing and dangled an arm casually over the back, observing with relish the change that had come over his young friend over the past few days. Her pale face had grown even paler, and there was a bluish cast to her skin, especially beneath her eyes.

She was anxious, filled with a kind of feverish expectancy that grew day by day. He'd noticed, stopping by every afternoon for a chat, that while she spoke less and less, she was becoming more and more charged with a kind of fierce single-mindedness.

"You know, when I was a student, I always liked the bus trip down to New York," he told her, locking his fingers behind his head, crossing his ankles comfortably. "Especially the morning bus. Leaving so early gives one such an overwhelming feeling of new beginnings. Oh—by the way—I can drop you by the bus station tomorrow morning if you'd like."

"Mom's going to . . . that's okay. She drives by it on her way to school," Kate answered vaguely.

He smiled. "Really quite the sudden reversal on her part, letting you go like this," he observed. "I'm glad for your sake. Finally being able to talk to your father. Have you given any more thought as to what you're going to say to him?"

Kate pulled herself up straight in the rocking chair, brushed a strand of hair from her cheek. "Well . . . I'm going to tell him . . . that they have to get back together again, but . . . he . . . I don't know if . . . what will I say if he says Mom won't go back?"

"Yesterday you said you thought she would," Nat reminded her. "That was you I was talking to here yesterday, wasn't it?"

Kate glanced across the porch to the sun-scorched lawn and to the pond shining in the late afternoon sun.

"I don't know . . ."

"Yesterday you were certain she would," Nat reminded her again, leaning forward in the porch swing.

"I think she would . . . if . . ." Kate looked distractedly down at her hands. "If she didn't have any choice."

"Between what, Kate? A choice between what?"

Kate looked at him, her eyes dark and reproachful. "You know what I mean."

Nat sat back in the porch swing, a smile stealing over his face. "So you're willing to be powerful," he said expansively. He praised her further: "After giving in so long to them, you're going to take the only option they've left you: to influence their lives with the threat of taking your own."

"I wouldn't really do it, though," Kate interjected.

"Kate, I know something about threats, and one thing I can tell you is that they don't work unless you absolutely believe you're capable of carrying them out."

She stood up from the rocking chair and walked to the other end of the porch. She looked out at the pond, her head bowed, her thin arms hanging at her sides. All at once, she turned back, facing Nat. "How long ago did you live in New York?"

"Oh . . . let me see . . . I guess about ten years ago. Why?"

"Because . . . maybe I saw you when I was . . . I sometimes feel like I met you."

Nat smiled. "You would have been about two years old, Kate."

"What if it doesn't work?"

"What?"

"What if, what if I say I don't want to live if they don't get back together and they don't believe me?"

"You'll cross that bridge when you come to it."

She cast him a glance out of the corner of her eye, looked away, then looked back again. "Sometimes you scare me."

He laughed. "Why should I scare you?"

"Because you . . . because we talk about terrible things sometimes."

"Good friends and good friendships are sometimes scary." He shrugged, still smiling.

Kate turned back to her contemplation of the pond. She had a different plan for her trip to New York, a plan that would ease her father more gently toward the resumption of their perfect New York life. She would consider using Nat's plan only if hers utterly failed.

"Did you hear me, Kate? I said good friendships are scary sometimes."

"I used to be so happy," Kate said. "And if . . . I have to, I *will* be happy again."

Nat smiled, leaned back and stretched his long legs. "That sounds like a solemn oath to me, Kate," he observed mildly. "An oath written in your own blood, if you will. Anything I can do to help, you just let me know."

'

12

BALLOWE: In your report you call the "squirrel incident" a complete success. But I'm unclear as to exactly why.

JASTER: I wanted her to think of herself as the squirrel, caught in a trap. With no way out but death. That was the purpose of the lesson.

BALLOWE: But I don't understand.

JASTER: Leverage. Her life as the lever. Unless her parents got back together, she would kill herself. Of course I led up

	to it slowly. And kept it all on a very hypothetical level.
BALLOWE:	But I still don't see the connection. The squirrel didn't commit suicide. You trapped him earlier, then killed him in front of the girl. It was murder, not suicide.
JASTER:	The girl had no framework—no way to think about death. I wanted her to see that death could be kind.
BALLOWE:	I'm still perplexed.
JASTER:	Excuse me, Demon Ballowe, but I thought you whisked me down here to commend me for my work. When I left her, she was preparing to carry out her threat after all—"
BALLOWE:	I'm just trying to clarify this for the committee, Jaster. Playing the devil's advocate, if you will. You wanted the girl to *threaten* suicide, and so you murdered a squirrel. If you could just fill in the blank for me, we'll move on.
JASTER:	I didn't really want her to just threaten suicide—I wanted her to think about it. On a subconscious level. I knew there was no chance her parents would

get back together—that her hopes would be disappointed—and I also suspected she would never have the meanness to actually threaten suicide—she didn't have a malicious bone in her body—but I knew she had the capacity for turning it inward. I had by then seen her large capacity for guilt and self-laceration, don't forget. She was a very inward girl and open to suggestion, as the subtraction strategy proved.

BALLOWE: A very deep strategy. How did the girl react to the killing of the squirrel?

JASTER: Driving back to her house, she decided we had done the right thing. When I heard that, I knew how close I was getting. I kept harping on the idea that the one great benefit of being human was the ability to make a choice about life. You didn't choose life, I told her, but you can choose when to leave life. We're not animals, I told her. We don't have to stupidly keep living if our lives become intolerable: suffering, like the squirrel, and then suffering some more. She had lost control over her life. Control is what I offered her. And power.

Finally, one day, all my innuendos and suggestions and observations paid off. She told me she had an idea. An idea about how to get her parents back together. I think I took it down verbatim in my report there, her exact words.

BALLOWE: Yes, you did.

JASTER: Would you mind reading it?

BALLOWE: *"If I told my father that unless he and my mom got married again, I'd kill myself, then they would have to listen to me."*

JASTER: Then the mother suddenly gave the girl her permission to go to New York and see her father. Another great opportunity, and time for another brilliant improvisation on my part. I began a new emergency phase in my attack— since she was going to New York, I seized on the trip as a kind of last showdown and portrayed it as such.

Naturally I worked to make the trip as disappointing and destructive as I possibly could.

You know the expression "for every cloud there is a silver lining"? Well, the reverse is also true, don't you think? For every silver lining, a cloud?

First, I told her how pleased I was for her. I emphasized over and over again how miraculous it was that she had been given the perfect opportunity to tell her father how she felt. Influence events. Use leverage. I reminded her how perfect it would be if her mother and father got remarried, and that she was the only one who could do it— once again: These were *her* thoughts. I was only echoing them back to her, building her hopes to a fever pitch.

BALLOWE: *Kate becomes more and more anxious. She sleeps little, talks to me only of how perfect her life would be if her parents were reunited and they all could live together in New York once more. I think she is getting ready, gath-*

ering her nerve to do something. I hope
it will be something self-destructive.

JASTER: At the same time I also reminded her
how imperfect her life would be if she
had to return to Black River. That was
the cloud she would have to return to.

You see, I wanted to push her to a
conclusion. Either New York and her
parents and perfection, or . . . nothing.
The void. And so I stoked this impossible dream for a week straight, fan-
ning the flames of her anxiety, her
hope, knowing all along that she didn't
have a chance to succeed. I was in a
state of high excitement myself. The
trip had given me a definite time frame
to work with. Because, of course, I
knew the real reason her father wanted
to see her. And so did her mother. As
a matter of fact, the only one who
didn't know was Kate.

13

"Any more of that General Po's chicken?"

Kate passed the carton to her father. Just looking at him was enough to make her happy—the long, thin face, his black hair mussed up and sticking out like he'd just woken up from a nap, his slow and deliberate way of speaking. Never in a hurry, her father lived in a kind of dreamy world, she thought.

"Did you notice anything different about the apartment?" she asked hopefully.

"The apartment?" he replied slowly. "Should I have?"

"Daddy—I cleaned it."

"You know I did notice it smelled nicer," he said pleasantly. "I thought maybe you were wearing perfume."

"Daddy—I never wear perfume."

"You know it *is* much cleaner," he said, looking around the kitchen, trying to make up for his earlier lack of appreciation.

"It's really nice being back in the city, Daddy," Kate said, changing the subject. "I really missed it."

He smiled at her, eyes crinkling at the corners. "You did? This nasty hot city?"

"It's not that hot."

"But the country's got those cool evenings. I don't suppose you brought any of those nice breezes with you?"

"No. Sorry."

"None in your knapsack? Oh well—there's always the air conditioner, I guess." He picked up his fork, speared a cube of glazed chicken.

Kate couldn't wait any longer; she had to ask him. After eight hours on the bus and then nearly five hours waiting in the apartment for him, her need to ask him about staying had become an almost physical craving.

"Will you excuse me just a minute, sweetie?" He got up from the kitchen table, asking her indulgence with a wry smile. "I've got to make a phone call—I just remembered something. Something I forgot to tell someone."

Kate looked down at her bowl, swirled the hot soup with a white plastic spoon. "Sure, Daddy." A few more minutes wouldn't matter, she decided. And besides, waiting was one of the things she did with her father. Other fathers might take their daughters shopping or to the movies; her father always sent her on ahead; she waited for him. It was just the way he was and one of the ways they were together.

Her worst wait so far that day had been in the Port Authority bus terminal, jammed with anxious commuters all in a rush to get home, briefcases swinging, wildly dodging through the wide halls. Adding to confusion, along the bright tiled walls, feet thrust out into the melée, were homeless men and women, begging. Their wild eyes, their sullen entreaties frightened Kate. She had always been scared of their desperation and misery, their threatening, half-human cries. But having to wait there among them for nearly an hour for her father to arrive, unable to simply walk past and ignore them, had been almost more than she could bear.

When she heard her name from a loudspeaker in the terminal—*"Katherine Whitson, please come to the security desk. Phone call for Katherine Whitson at the security desk"*—she'd breathed a sigh of relief. It would be her father, running late, calling to apologize, calling to send her down to his apartment to wait. "I'm really sorry, Katie—can you meet me at the apartment?" he'd said, his voice sounding very close in the earpiece at the information booth. "I'm in the middle of something here and—do you still have your key? Great—I'll be down there around six—I swear. Then we'll go out to that nice little Italian place you like so much."

Threading her way downstairs to the subway through the throngs of bumping commuters, she'd felt suddenly buoyant, as if she might float away. The unhappiness, the loneliness of the past two months all at once seemed to evaporate: She was finally going to see her father. She hadn't been able to subtract him when she left and now she knew why—she loved him too much.

The subway was an oven, the train stuffed with sweating, shoving passengers, but she'd been filled with a sense of belonging, a feeling of home so over-whelming that for a moment she could barely breathe for joy: the excitement and tension and terror of New York City, her perfect New York. Across the platform she'd watched the uptown train take on its passengers knowing that she could board that train and be standing in Dr. Kelly's office within half an hour, playing Ping-Pong and drinking iced tea with him, Bach cantatas blasting from his old record player. Coming up out of the subway onto Fourteenth Street, she'd felt more clear-eyed and alive than she had in months.

Turning onto Tenth, her father's street, she had an inspiration. Instead of waiting to be taken to Arturo's she would order Chinese food, warm it in the oven, then serve him dinner when he got home. He loved Chinese food, and she could talk to him better in the quiet apartment than in the clanging, festive restaurant.

Climbing the six narrow flights of stairs with the aromatic bag of take-out food, she'd savored each worn marble step, recalling it from memory. At his door, she felt the cool air seeping out from under the door onto her ankles, remembered the many times she'd stood waiting for him to unlock the door and take her in his arms. She smiled at her nostalgia, then let herself into the chilly apartment, closing her eyes with pleasure as the refrigerated air washed over her.

Taking her sky blue memo pad out of her knapsack, turning to the page marked "Dad," she looked at all the things she'd subtracted two months before: the rolltop desk, the books, the TV, the table lamps still on the floor. She tore out the page, crumpled it into a tight prickly ball, then carried it into the kitchen and burned it to ash on top of the stove.

Next, she called Chuan Lee. Chuan, her gentle voice so polite, gave Kate another thrill of belonging. Kate told Chuan that she was in New York, about her bus trip, then, her heart beating in her throat, asked if she could come stay for a week starting on Monday.

When Chuan's mother got on the phone, Kate lied and said her father had given his permission. And your mother? Mrs. Lee asked. She says it's fine, too, Kate lied. We'd love to have you, Mrs. Lee said. Have your father call me later.

She got out the vacuum cleaner, thoroughly vacuumed the entire apartment, spending extra time under the bed, getting all the dust balls. Next she'd mopped and waxed the kitchen floor. While it dried, she took a can of spray polish and a rag and rubbed it energetically into his desk, the old mirrored headboard on the bed, the coffee table. She did the bathroom last, spraying cleanser on the tiles, scouring the toilet, and scrubbing the bathtub until everything was bright and gleaming. As she worked she thought about him coming home and seeing how good it would be if she stayed with him.

If her father would only say yes to the first thing and let her stay with Chuan. Then would come the second part of her plan: When he came back from his trip, she would talk to him about her staying in New York.

"Just a little thing I had to clear up, sweetie," her father said, coming back into the kitchen. "I've got such a lot of loose ends I've to take care of these days."

Kate, sitting forward over the table, gathered her nerve and asked, "Daddy, can I stay for an extra week? I already talked to Chuan Lee and Mrs. Lee, and they say I can stay with them until you get back."

"Oh? Well . . . I . . . I don't know, Kate. . . ." Her father blinked in surprise. "I suppose. But have you talked to your mother about this?"

"I only thought of it on the way down."

"Well, I don't know. . . ."

"And then I could stay with you when you come back from your trip?" she said hopefully. "Just for another week?"

"Well . . . I . . . to tell you the truth, things are going to be a little crazy around here in a few days . . . there's going to be . . . I mean I'd love to have you stay and . . . um, everything . . . but . . ."

He touched his wine glass at the stem and rotated it between his fingertips, suddenly intent on the red liquid as it sloshed slowly around.

"Katie—actually—this is hard—well, because see,

Katie, I'm going to be packing up the apartment that week because my boss, Dr. Mead, has decided, well, I've been asked to head up a new research division in Atlanta so I won't be . . . I'll be moving in September."

She stared at her father, not quite understanding.

"It's a big promotion," he went on, sitting a bit straighter in his chair, still staring at the wine. "And it'll mean big things for me, I hope. They've been after me for months to make a decision, and now with you and your mom, um, gone, I felt before I couldn't go and be a good father at the same time, so I put them off . . . but now . . ."

Suddenly it all made horrible sense to Kate: He had asked her to come down to tell her this.

"You can come see me in Atlanta anytime you want. . . ." he went on. "It's a very nice city, Atlanta. I went down two weeks ago to look at houses and I've got one picked out—a three-bedroom job—so you can come stay anytime you want. And I've got a buyer for this place. Your mother and I haven't worked out all the details yet, but I'd like you to stay with me next summer. . . ."

She looked up into the corner of the ceiling, trying to catch her breath. "Mom knew. . . ."

He looked at her blankly for a moment. "Knew what?"

"That you were going to tell me this. . . ."

"Well, yes, sweetie, of course."

His words were like a curtain, closing against her, a shroud of words that meant there was no hope, that she would never come back to New York, never be able to come back to her perfect life. She exploded. *"But Daddy! You can't! You can't leave me!"*

"But Katie," he said, recoiling in surprise. "I'm not leaving you—you can stay with me in the summer and come down any weekend you want—"

"But you need to be in New York! I want you to be here!"

"Now . . . um, Katie, settle down . . . I'm just moving to Atlanta . . . and . . ."

"But I want to stay here and go to school!" Kate said. "And be with Chuan Lee. And Dr. Kelly. And have everything back the way it was! I'll be good—I won't, you won't make me—I'll stay here with you!"

"Well, gee, Katie . . . that's . . . you know . . . I'm afraid it's—Your mom . . . Your mom wants you to live in the country where it's safer, and I agree with her there."

"But Daddy!"

"Honey—I thought you liked living in the country," he said, almost pleading with her. "In your letters you said—I got the impression—"

"I want to come back here!" Kate insisted. "I want everything back the way it was! I want you and Mommy to get back together. And move back to the house—"

She'd said it. Finally told her father her deepest wish. She knew immediately from her father's expression that it could never happen. And she heard how ridiculous her wish really was.

He shifted uncomfortably in his chair. "Now Katie—wait just a minute—you're beginning to sound . . ."

"You can just quit your job and get another one here," Kate went on, risking everything. "In New York. And then Mom can come down, and we could be a family again!"

"Oh . . . jeez, Katie—I had no idea," he said slowly. "I mean . . . I'm very lucky to have been offered this job, Kate, and I had no idea . . . it means I'll be able to send you to a good private college . . . and . . ."

"But Daddy! I don't care about that!"

"But . . . Kate—the house in Atlanta is—I already signed a commitment. I have to move out of here by September first." His face grew solemn. "So what you're asking . . . and this business with your mother . . . that could never happen . . . I know you're a little homesick—your mom told me . . . but . . .

you'll be fine . . . really . . . once you get started in school and everything, don't you think?"

"But Daddy, if you don't, if you don't—I'll—we have to—I have to live here—or else—"

She broke off; couldn't say it, couldn't make the threat about killing herself. It all seemed so stupid suddenly. Stupid and hopeless. Everything was gone. It was over.

"Kate—I know it's been hard for you, what with everything that's happened between your mom and me, but . . . well . . . one thing I agree with your mother on is that we have to get on with our lives. You have to get on with yours, too, and . . . give it a chance."

Kate stared down at her plateful of rice. *Daddy − Daddy = 0. Daddy − Kate = 0. Kate − Kate = 0. Subtraction. A simple, terrible thing.*

14

The next morning, Saturday, she left the apartment while her father was taking his shower. Without telling him, without leaving a note, taking her backpack; it was a small gesture of revenge.

She got on the uptown subway, following no particular plan. Columbus Circle was the place she got off, at the bottom of Central Park. She stood for a time beside the looming statue of Christopher Columbus, considering where she would go next; eventually the hot sun, honking taxis, and acrid bus fumes drove her into the park.

She followed a wide asphalt path through a grove of stunted trees. On either side, scattered on the green benches, homeless men and women slept awkwardly, as if they had fallen exhausted in the night and had not the strength to move. Their presence irritated Kate. They made her feel uncomfortable and vaguely guilty. For a moment, she considered taking the blue notebook out of her knapsack and subtracting the homeless people, but instead she kept her eyes straight ahead and eliminated them by shutting them out of her mind.

Deeper into the park the sounds of the city, sifted through the leaves, were suppressed, the odd bark of a car horn puncturing the rush of traffic, the incidental hum of millions of lives. Soon the path emptied into a spacious, rolling lawn. There sunbathers, radios hissing and clucking, were scattered across the green expanse. A humid haze, dense along the trees, hung over the sun worshipers. They did not look at all real to Kate, more like washed manikins drying in the sun. Weaving in and out of the prone bodies, a crew of screaming children were throwing a football, giggling if it bounced too close to a sunbather, exploding with glee when the ball took an odd bounce and hit someone.

How much farther was the pond, that cool, sensible oval? For there, she realized, was where she wanted to go. Before she had always taken the subway up to Seventy-seventh Street; she'd never walked up from the bottom of the park. So which path would take her to the reflecting pool? There were five emptying into the lawn, flowing in from all directions. Why didn't I take the subway there in the first place, she asked herself angrily. Why don't I ever know what I want until it's too late?

Stepping from the shaded path into the hot blast of sun, she walked to the closest sunbather, a white-skinned young woman in bright plaid shorts and a black tank top. Eyes closed, the woman was listening to music, tiny black discs plugged into her ears, squirming to a beat only she could hear.

"Excuse me."

The woman's eyes flicked open, then with showy disgust she shut off the small tape recorder on her stomach. "Yeah?"

"Do you—can you tell me the best way to get to the reflecting pool?"

She jerked a thumb. "It's over there someplace."

"But . . . isn't there a path that goes—"

"Yeah. I told you. Over there someplace." The woman flicked on her music and began squirming again, singing in an off-key rasp: "Dreamer . . . love me, love me now."

Kate retreated to the shade, staring over her shoulder, wishing she could have said something to match the woman's mean disinterest. She even imagined going back and revenging herself with a few sharp words, but rejected the idea. The pool—that was what she wanted. Now where was it? Why was it so hot? The pool was on the east side, but how much farther? She was suddenly weak, drained and shaky in the heat.

Smelling smoke, she saw a souvlaki vendor selling his food and drink on the northeast corner of the lawn, a jagged line of customers snaking out from the chrome cart. A soda, that's what I need, she decided. Something cold. Her father always used to buy her a soda at the reflecting pool. Her father . . . she didn't want to think about her father. Was he still in the shower? No, he would be out by now, padding around the apartment barefoot in his saggy blue bathrobe, wondering where she was, waiting for her to come back. How many hours would she make him wait? What would be fair? A hundred hours? A thousand? A billion?

By the time she crossed the steamy lawn, the line at the cart had dwindled to two teenage girls. Dressed in long white T-shirts, black sandals, and sunglasses, they were talking loudly about some boy named Alan.

"He thinks he's so cool," the first girl said, carelessly holding out a limp dollar bill to the vendor.

"The only reason I go out with him is his money," the other girl said with a shrug. "He takes me nice places. He *is* a real dweeb, but don't worry, I'm going to dump him when school starts."

"Hey—don't you live in my building?"

The remark was directed at Kate. Two pairs of black lenses goggled at her.

"I . . . I used to live in Brooklyn."

"Oh—" The taller girl shook her head. "Sorry." She turned to her friend. "But doesn't she look like the girl—you know the one I'm talking about—"

Her friend suddenly shrieked with laughter. "Oh, that one! I know the one—she does—how funny!"

And that's what Mom wants me to be like, Kate thought with a snort, watching the girls stroll off. Talking about boys and thinking about boys and being part of a clique and getting contact lenses so boys will like me.

"Next!" shouted the vendor. He was a short, stooped man with bulbous eyes and a purplish dime-sized wart in the center of his forehead. "Who's next?" he yelled, waving a long fork, mopping his upper lip with a paper napkin. "Hey, you want somethin'? Hey—you—hot dog?"

She stepped into the shade beneath the vendor's yellow umbrella. "A soda. A grape soda."

He thrust his hand into a compartment, pulled out a purple can, popped it open, stuck in a straw, and handed it to her.

"Can you tell me where the reflecting pool is?"

"One dollar," he said sullenly.

Kate dug a crumpled bill from her pocket. "Can you tell me where the reflecting pool is?"

He glared at her, his eyes suddenly dark and furious. "I look like a map to you? I sell soda. I don't know nothin'. Next! Next!"

The fury that had been building in Kate all morning finally rose to her lips. "You do too," she shot back, losing control. "You do too know where it is!"

"One dollar. Give me a dollar."

Kate, her hand shaking, held out the can. "Take it back. I don't want it. Take it back."

The vendor grinned, the wart on his forehead bulging luridly. "Too late. It's already open. One dollar."

"I hate you!" Kate shouted, flinging her dollar bill into the vendor's face, her sudden savagery catching him completely off guard. He shrank back, blinking, his mouth working in silent surprise.

Kate turned and fled for the trees. She fully expected the man to run after her, even imagined him stabbing her with his fork. When nothing happened, she chanced a look over her shoulder and saw he was dumbly staring after her. The novelty of the situation—someone being afraid of her for once—touched Kate in a peculiar way: She laughed. Nat was always talking about power, about seizing control. Well, she had finally done it and he was right: It felt good.

At the edge of the treeline, she stopped and sucked at the soda straw, enjoyed the sweet grapey carbonation fizzing and popping along her gums. Soda had never tasted this good before, she decided. To the victor goes the spoils—that's what Nat would say. She laughed again, the same wild, vengeful laugh that had come out before. A laugh she found both frightening and exhilarating.

Almost immediately, she felt her stomach clench in shock as the cold, sweet liquid hit bottom. Gasping, she fought the twitching, humiliating signals in her stomach. So stupid, she thought. Icy cold soda on a hot day—so stupid. As stupid as believing her father would let her stay in New York. That her parents would get back together. As stupid as thinking that yelling at some man in the park could change anything. What kind of power was that? It was hollow; it was nothing.

She flung the soda can to the ground and ran blindly into the trees.

Queasy, disheveled, her pale face flushed with exertion, she came out of the wooded area some fifteen minutes later and found herself at the top of a small, grass-covered hill. At the bottom, she recognized the curving asphalt path that led to the south entrance of the reflecting pool. The pool—what was the point? Why had she come? I subtracted this months ago, she thought. This is already gone. The park, the trees, the pool. Why am I here? You came here to say good-bye, a voice told her. This is the end.

Yet everywhere she looked there was bright activity: young parents pushing strollers; couples walking arm in arm; bicyclists whizzing past on winking, flashing wheels. One person in particular caught her attention: an old woman sitting on a bench wearing a broad-brimmed straw, her head tipped back, face peaceful and composed in the sunshine. It was Miss Peel, wasn't it? Whoever she was, she looked just like her.

Striding stiff-legged down the hill, Kate decided she would make sure it wasn't Miss Peel. It was ridiculous and foolish, she knew—the woman looked less and less like her as Kate got closer—but it was something she had to do.

Before she could get close enough to make absolutely sure, Kate came across a young woman, sprawled half on the grass, half on the asphalt path, a soiled coffee cup with a few cents in the bottom clutched in her hand. Asleep or exhausted, cheeks rouged up to an unnatural pink, a black pillbox hat with a torn veil pinned low on her forehead, wearing a short black dress that exposed angry red sores on her legs, the woman looked as if she'd been at a party, but that something terrible had happened to her, as if she'd gotten lost or had been beaten up or had gone insane and never made it home, and now would never make it home. The vivid makeup, the peculiar clothing—Kate couldn't walk past; she felt rooted to the spot.

And then, all at once, Kate had an extraordinary impulse. The longer she stood there, looking down, the more powerful and frightening the feeling became. She felt that if she could make herself lie down beside the woman, hold the woman in her arms, that somehow, some part of herself would be changed forever. She was scared of the feeling, scared of what it could mean. It didn't make any sense.

People were staring at her. One older man, holding a little white dog on a leash, screwed up his face and muttered something about common decency, not staring at the unfortunate.

Kate circled around behind the woman onto the grass, each step growing more and more difficult. At length, hating the feeling and surrendering to it, she knelt down, and tentatively, her hand shaking, reached out to touch the woman's arm. Before she could, the woman rolled over onto her back, her eyes moving in a rapid frenzy beneath her eyelids. Whimpering, she scratched at the filthy sores on her arms.

All at once the image of the dying squirrel leapt into Kate's mind. She's trapped, Kate thought. Trapped just like the squirrel. Just as she had been trapped three months before in her bedroom, when her mother told her they were moving to a new life in the country. She'd be better off just dying, Kate thought, standing and looking down at the woman. Better dead and out of her misery. Shocked at herself for thinking such a horrible thing, Kate turned away and ran toward the reflecting pool.

When Kate reached her favorite bench by the Hans Christian Andersen statue, she tried to push the image of the woman out of her mind. There was Hans over his book, she reassured herself; there was the little bronze girl sitting frozen on his knee, never knowing the end of the story, the big bronze book stuck on the same page for eternity, just like always.

Kate sat down and stared at the shimmering water,

the white concrete apron battering her eyes. *And their eyes shall be bathed in heavenly light.* Who said that? Miss Peel? What about the pink-rouged woman in the torn party dress? Would her eyes be bathed in heavenly light, too? Or would she be subtracted? Subtraction—that simple, beautiful thing. Who would subtract her? God? What about all the people who walked past without offering help? Would He subtract them, too?

Ten feet in front of her, a little redheaded boy in a white sailor suit tentatively placed his sailboat in the water, then pushed it out into the pond. His parents, offering encouragement, stood proudly beside him. Just as her own parents had done, back when she was little and life was perfect.

She felt like running over to the boy and saying: "Remember this always, little boy. Remember the water, the warm sun smooth on your face, remember your feelings pure and clean, how much you loved your little boat and how much your parents loved you."

"Looks nice and cool, doesn't it?"

A youngish woman in a sundress sat down beside her on the bench. A fragrance, flowery and soft, filled the air about her.

"Be nice to be able to go for a swim, wouldn't it?"

"I can't swim . . ." Kate replied after a long moment. She didn't want to talk.

"Well, for a wade then," the woman said, with a small laugh. "Roll up your pants and go for a nice wade."

Kate stood. "Um, I've got to get going."

"Oh, sorry—did I upset your meditations? I'm sorry," the woman said attentively. "I didn't mean to."

"No . . . I was just um, saying good-bye . . . um, good-bye to this . . ."

The woman stood, smiled sympathetically, reached out, and touched Kate's hand. "Oh . . . then I did butt in . . . I'm so sorry. You stay, dear. I'm sorry to have bothered you."

Her dress billowing in the breeze, the woman walked around to the other side of the pool and sat down on a bench by the boathouse. It was terrible, Kate thought, that a stranger could be kinder than either one of her parents. Kate wished the woman would come back. She wanted to tell her about saying good-bye. She had started to, but something had stopped her.

What had stopped her? What had stopped her from lying down in the grass beside the poor lost woman? Fear of people's opinions? Shame? Being frightened

122
≋

of where those thoughts and feelings would lead? Subtracting herself when her feelings grew too strong?

She unslung her knapsack from her shoulder, unzipped the flap, and took out her wallet. Thirty-two dollars. Kate would give it to the woman. She stuffed the money into the front pocket of her jeans and walked out the way she'd come.

The soiled coffee cup with its few miserable pennies was still there; the woman was gone, the imprint of her body still fresh in the grass. Subtraction. Subtraction was everywhere. Kate knelt down in the grass and closed her eyes. Subtraction—a simple, beautiful thing—that's what Nat believed. Like the man in the library.

But wasn't addition a beautiful thing, too? What if before leaving New York three months before she had *added* everything together in her notebook. Added and even multiplied the special places and people, day by day, until her notebook was a treasure trove of memories, safely hoarded.

But that was wrong, too, she thought, shaking her head slowly, thinking hard. Both ways, subtracting and adding, implied a solution, the end of a process, a death, stasis.

The universe wasn't static. The universe was always

in a process of becoming, blossoming, dying. Stars and suns burned out, galaxies came and went; the universe spun on, churning toward another gathering of light, of energy, a bright burning knot poised for the touch of creation.

Just as she had been touched. Touched first by the terrible dream of the burning water, then the sight of the woman in the grass, then the kindness of the fragrant young woman by the pool.

Somehow she knew these things were bound up in one another, that they partook of the same mystery. And she knew, and it frightened her, that if she'd lain down with the woman in the grass she might have known what it was, might have understood more of that mystery.

I'm homeless too, Kate thought, standing. The only difference is I have a ticket on a bus.

As the long miles wore into the gathering night, as the gently rocking bus climbed into the Catskill Mountains, Kate fell asleep, her head wedged between the edge of the seat and window, and dreamed half-awake, half-asleep dreams. One moment, the trees on the side of the highway were rushing by, and the next, she was standing on a subway platform, dark trains hurtling past, red lights glowing, blue sparks flashing beneath the wheels. In one of the dreams Miss Peel and Ezra were holding open a subway door, shouting to the people on the platform as the train raced past.

Exhausted, she arrived in Black River near midnight, finding it deserted and cold and drizzling and blanketed with mist. She was the only passenger who disembarked from the bus; the driver, morose, smelling of coffee, let her out without a word.

She called her mother from the pay phone beside the locked and lightless aluminum trailer that served as the town's bus station, shivering there in the open booth in her white shorts and white summer shirt. She found her mother frantic with worry, a worry that became anger when she found her daughter was safe, close by. Her father had called. They were both very angry with her. "You're never to do something like this again," her mother told her.

Hanging up the receiver, Kate found she didn't care. What was the difference, really? Weren't they the ones who had run away? Run away from her?

She sat down on the rough wooden bench alongside the trailer, stepping over a wide, black puddle that lay like a moat in front of it. Seated on the hard slats, she watched the rain prick at the surface of the puddle, the orange light from a streetlight wobbling across the center.

Dully, she closed her eyes. The rouged woman sprawled across her thoughts, vivid, followed by a picture of her father's soft, puzzled betrayal in the bright kitchen. For one unsettling moment, she felt as if her mind were working entirely on its own, spinning and churning up warped shards of memory, mixing everything together, blending them with her strange dreams on the bus.

She would talk to Nat, she decided. Tell him about the homeless woman and the yearning she'd had to lie down with her. Would he understand? Or would he say the words about choosing death, choosing it bravely? It was sometimes so hard to know what he would say.

She stared into the black puddle. Her old life—her perfect life—had passed away. She was the only part of the dream that was left: the dreamer. Everything else was gone.

15

The headlights of Nat Worthy's red pickup swept across the rain black lot, skimming across the gleaming asphalt; at last Kate was caught in their beam. Her thin shoulders hunched against the drizzle, she did not look up.

Setting the footbrake with a low rasp, Nat Worthy took time to study her. He watched her stand up, squint awkwardly into the headlights, snatch up her knapsack from the bench, lay it down again, squint perplexedly into the beams. She appeared to be confused, worried. He spent a few more moments observing her anxiety before shutting down the ignition, killing the headlights, and stepping out of the truck.

Kate grabbed the strap of her knapsack once more, straddled the puddle in front of the bench, stepped over it, and took a step toward the truck. But then, instead of walking the ten or so feet to meet Nat, she stopped and waited for Nat to come to her. For it was Nat; she was sure of that now.

She had thought at first it was her mother's car. Sensing the lights from the first, she had not looked until the last possible moment, unwilling to let go of the tide of resolve that was welling up inside her.

Kate had been thinking: Ever since the move from New York, her mother's expressed wish had been to know exactly what she was feeling. Sitting there waiting in the summer drizzle, she'd felt strongly that the time had come to answer her mother, and to do so more fully than she suspected her mother actually would want.

The few times Kate had told her mother of her feelings—the afternoon in the church parking lot, the day of her terrible nightmare—she had given improper names to her emotions, hiding their true nature from her mother, from herself. Despair and anger: She had called these loneliness. Her sense of betrayal and loss: She had talked of perfect worlds and begged to go back to New York. She was angry with herself for not having been honest. And so, when she did look up into the headlights, it was with the promise to herself that she would not speak falsely to her mother on this night.

Looking up, seeing that it was not her mother who had come to get her, but Nat Worthy instead, his shoulders straight and proud and swaggering as he alighted from the truck, she assumed her mother had sent him in her place. At first she was thankful for the delay; she could think through her feelings once more on the drive home before confronting her mother, but an instant later, watching him approach, she realized with some anxiety that she hadn't had time to think through precisely the things she wanted to say to him. And her resolve, her sense of mastery, faltered.

He stood before her, wearing his brick red sport coat, the very one he'd worn the first day he'd come by to meet her. Now as he looked down at her, his face was lined with concern, even disapproval.

"Oh—Nat—hi," she said, flustered. "How are you? Did my mom send you?"

"How was the trip, Kate?" he asked, without returning her greeting. "Did it go well for you? Will you be moving back to New York now?"

She pushed her glasses back up on her nose and looked past his shoulder. Of course he would want to know about that. Of course he'd want to know if she'd won the day in New York. He wouldn't know how little that seemed to matter now; he saw things in absolutes: win or lose, empty or full, perfection or destruction. How could she describe those awful, searing minutes in the park or what they meant? She suspected, no, she *knew* Nat would never understand.

"Well . . . no . . . my father is moving away," she said, stating the facts. "He's going to Atlanta."

He gave her a long, penetrating look, not speaking.

"They talked about it before I even went," Kate went on softly. "That's why my mother let me go. So he could tell me."

"Your mother didn't send me, Kate," he said, drily answering her question. "I had a feeling you'd be back tonight. I had a feeling you'd give in to weakness."

"He already bought the house and everything. He never—" Kate broke off, thinking: Why am I apologizing?

"What did you say to him?" Nat asked, pressing closer. "Did you give him your ultimatum?"

Kate looked into his eyes, searching for a glimmer of the understanding that she had so often found there.

Perhaps she could explain about the park, about the woman in the grass.

He leaned closer, his voice lowering into a deep, unfamiliar register: "Kate—seeing you here tonight, I knew you didn't have the courage to make the ultimatum to your father: your life or your happiness. Because if you had, you'd never have had to come back here. You'd be in New York. Living the life you want to live."

"But Nat—really—there was nothing I could do. It was already, it wasn't—" She stopped, disgusted with her fear of his opinion. "But Nat, something happened," she began again. "I went to the park and there was a homeless woman there. Homeless people always used to scare me, but because I saw that, in a way, I didn't have a home either, I had this feeling I should lie down next to her. But I didn't, I stopped, because I was afraid—I thought about the squirrel and what you said about being miserable. I think, Nat, you were wrong. I mean I didn't want to look when you killed it, but I should have because—"

"When you said you were going to take control of your life, I respected you, Kate," he said, interrupting her. "But apparently you succumbed to weakness. You are weak and cowardly. And there is no room in my life for cowards."

131
≈

Had he really just said such a terrible thing to her? Kate looked down at the black, gleaming asphalt and struggled to catch her breath. Maybe there *had* been a moment in her father's kitchen when she might have seized control of her life with the threat of suicide. But what kind of life would that have been? Holding her father hostage under the threat of her own subtraction.

"But Nat . . . why . . . why are you being so . . . so . . . mean to me?" she managed to bring out at last.

He regarded her with a thin, unyielding smile. "I have news of my own, Kate. I'm leaving Black River. I've been offered a job, a full professorship at a small teacher's college in Oregon. Yes, Katie, I'm leaving. And very soon. Day after tomorrow. I have to get there and get started with planning the course work. They're in a big hurry to get me out there."

He straightened to his full height. "So tell me, Kate, what are you going to do now? What are you going to do to change *your* life?"

"But Nat—it wouldn't have worked," Kate pleaded, growing more and more upset with herself for wanting to hold onto him, to please him, to explain herself to him. "I was going to say it—I almost did—but I knew there was . . . I could tell there was no way. I ran away. I ran away up to the park without telling him and—"

"You'll always run away, Kate," Nat cut in. "You'll never have the courage to do what you must."

"I will! I will, Nat! I already do, Nat—listen!"

"No, Kate—you came back here; nothing is solved. Your chance for a perfect life in New York is gone. What is left for you? What are you going to do now?"

She dared to look into his eyes again. There was something cold and relentless in those eyes, implacable, prideful, which only saw one solution for her.

She took a step backward, accidentally splashing into the cold, black puddle behind her. For one strangely sweet moment, she hid in the sensation of the cool water on her ankles.

"What are you going to do now, Kate? Your perfect life is gone forever."

Perfection, infinity, eternity. The bright numbers gathered up into the light, the numinous light which drew them up and spewed them out, transformed. Would God gather her up? The woman in the park with the terrible sores, would God gather her up like the numbers into the light, the bright, burning knot poised for his touch of creation?

Yes. But Nat would rather she die. Nat would rather

everything die. Suddenly, irrevocably, she saw the dark landscape of their friendship illuminated, thrown into bleak relief as if by brilliant and fearful lightning. She saw back to the first days of their friendship, saw that his evil intention had been there all along. She saw forward to the end of his equation: After the subtraction, that perfect, terrible thing, the solution: nothingness, her nothingness, his exultation at her nothingness. And when she saw that, a burning chip of ice pierced her heart; a drop of his malice leavened her blood.

She opened her eyes again, thinking, How would it be if he were my equation? Watching him closely, she said the words he wanted her so much to say: "I'm going to kill myself."

And she saw something in those eyes, for the briefest flicker, a gleam like a bright fish leaping into the air, a flash so furtive and pleased that it sent a chill prickling through her neck.

"But you didn't make the threat to your father," he remarked. "It doesn't mean anything unless you made the threat."

"It will mean I won't have to live anymore," she replied, matching his quiet, insinuating tone of voice.

"And do you really think killing yourself is the answer, Kate?"

Strangely, she felt like laughing. All this time she had

134
≈

thought him a friend, a friend who wasn't afraid to say exactly what he thought. Now she saw that all of it—the talks on the porch, the drives in the backwoods—had been leading to this moment. That she had almost been a perfect fool.

"Do you want to know how I'm going to do it?" she asked, drawing him in, leading him the same way he had led her. "I'm going to drown myself in that pond beside the house. I'm going to walk in until the water is over my head and keep walking until the water is so deep I can't walk back. I'm going to do it at dawn."

He nodded soberly. "You seem to have given this a great deal of thought. I feel honored that you've shared your plans with me. Only a true friend would tell. . . ."

"Actually, I just thought of it."

She enjoyed his raised eyebrows, his surprise at her casual reply. But perhaps she'd gone too far. "I'd like to be alone now," she said. "If you don't mind."

"I was going to offer you a ride home. Would that . . ."

"No—I'm really, I really should wait for my mother."

"Of course. Of course you should."

"Good luck at your new job, Nat."

"Well . . . yes . . . thank you and . . . good-bye, Kate. It's been a pleasure knowing you."

"Good-bye, Nat."

He bent slightly at the waist, spun on his toes and walked tall and proud to his truck. She watched him all the way, watched him pull into the rain-slicked street, saw his eyes in the rearview mirror as he passed under a streetlight, avid, bright, without mercy.

She took up her knapsack from the bench and drew it on over her shoulders. Following an impulse of joy, she turned and jumped with both feet into the cold, black puddle. She threw her head back, the thin drizzle stinging her cheeks, and laughed so hard that burning tears filled her eyes.

16

BALLOWE: What did you think when you saw her
           tear out and burn that page from her
           notebook in her father's kitchen?

JASTER: Oh—I was very pleased to see that. She
           thought she was free, she thought she
           could undo the subtractions with a
           symbolic act. She didn't yet know that
           she was the one who was about to be
           subtracted. She didn't know that her
           one safe haven was about to be de-
           stroyed.

BALLOWE: You had known about the father's new job all along, of course.

JASTER: Yes, of course, I had been keeping tabs on her father's situation for months. Eventually I knew he would take the job in Atlanta. He would feel guilty about it, being so far away from his daughter, but he didn't have any real qualms about moving. In his own mealy-mouthed way he is just as much a careerist as his wife. There was no reason for him to stay in New York anymore.

So it was perfect—I'd kept her living in the past, in a doomed fantasy that I cultivated throughout the summer. I kept her in the past, or focused her on the future, never letting her focus on the present.

You see, I knew that she couldn't actually go through with the "subtraction threat." She was incapable of that kind of manipulative behavior. But she was more than capable of turning her feelings inward. And therefore primed for the taking of her own life—which

≋

I'd like very much to witness. Are we nearly through here?

BALLOWE: Nearly. You are nearly through. Just a few minutes more should do it. But this is all very illuminating, Jaster. You quite obviously think yourself a master at this kind of deep game.

JASTER: Thank you. But really, it's rather easy once you've done it a few times.

BALLOWE: So you've used these unorthodox methods before, then.

JASTER: Oh yes—I've been experimenting ever since I started in the field.

BALLOWE: Fifteen years ago. Well, you certainly are something of a maverick, I must say.

JASTER: Well, as I said before, I don't want to be a field operative forever.

BALLOWE: Oh, I don't think you'll be an operative much longer, Jaster. Not after the work you've done here.

JASTER: Thank you.

BALLOWE: And so the girl went home to Black River.

JASTER: Yes. Despondent. Crushed. Completely crushed.

BALLOWE: And you spoke to her.

JASTER: Yes. Last night. I saw that the time had
             come to deliver the final blow. I ar-
             ranged to "run into her" at the bus
             station in order to give her a push
             down the final spiral of despair. I told
             her she was a failure. I told her our
             friendship was over. I told her I was
             moving the next day. I tell you, the
             look of despair in her eyes was abso-
             lutely priceless. Her best friend, her
             wise counselor rebuking her, leaving
             her forever, just like her father. She was
             done for.

BALLOWE: Complete despair—how could you
             tell?

JASTER: You come to recognize these symptoms
             after a while.

BALLOWE: Oh yes—your vast experience—I for-
             got.

JASTER: Are you . . . are you mocking me?

BALLOWE: Oh no—Hell forbid. I wouldn't dream
             of mocking one so brilliant. Tell me,
             Jaster, did it ever cross your mind that
             the girl might be lying to you? That she

only told you what you wanted to hear?

JASTER: What? What do you mean? What possible reason—

BALLOWE: That possibly she was, in her own way, testing you?

JASTER: Don't be ridiculous. I saw the look in her eyes. She was ready to die. And—what is all this anyway? Let me go back; we can all go back and watch my final triumph.

BALLOWE: Or maybe, just maybe, Jaster, she wasn't ready to die but instead saw who you really are. Hell knows you'd dropped enough clues by then.

JASTER: Nonsense. What are you talking about?

BALLOWE: The dawn has come and gone on earth, Jaster. And because of your idiocy and insubordination we're going to be short one soul down here in Hell. That's what I'm talking about.

17

The sun rose, glowing a fiery orange at the horizon as Kate looked out her bedroom window. She stood there for five long minutes, watching the morning mist shroud the pond in a vaporous mantle.

Turning from the window, Kate quietly pulled open her dresser drawer, took out jeans and white socks, and then went to the closet for her tennis shoes. From there she also took her white windbreaker. She slipped out of her nightgown and dressed. In the mirror, she looked like an apparition, radiant in the soft light.

Before leaving her room, she took the sky blue memo pad from her knapsack.

She crept down the long upstairs hall silently, careful not to make a sound, so as not to wake her mother. Pausing at the top step for a moment, remembering the first day Nat Worthy had come to visit, she took a deep breath, then quietly descended to the landing and slipped out onto the porch.

The air was moist, shot through with the scent of grass and dew. The last chitterings of the crickets, the creak and mutter of the oaks along Keener Road: How solemn and precious was the end of the night.

She walked across the side lawn into the thick, wet saw grass surrounding the pond, the rank, sour odor growing more and more palpable, a bitter taste at the back of her throat.

She came to the muddy edge, the mist swirling around to her waist. Turning, she looked a long time at the white frame house glowing orange in the growing light, her recent path through the long grass a dark, pensive slash. Beyond the house, the deep sky was opening, cerulean, ready to accept the coming of the day.

Bending to touch the pond with her fingertips, she discovered the water was warm. Pushing the algae aside with the toe of her sneaker, she made an opening, then slowly, a little squeamish, waded into the muck, the water spilling into her shoes, sinking into the ooze.

As the rancid water reached her waist, she stopped and listened. She hoped Nat was watching. It would be like him to lurk close by, observing. She stretched her senses until she became aware of a kind of rapt buzzing in the mist. She felt sure he was close.

Opening the sky blue notebook to the first page—the subtraction of the too-bright pizza parlor, the dark subway platform—she flipped through until she reached the last of the subtractions, then, with a sudden forceful rip, wrenched the pages from the wire spiral, small bits of paper fluttering about her face like confetti.

Folding the equations in half, she drew her arm back and all at once slung the pages into the air, watching them telescope open, separate, and flutter out in every direction before settling on the surface, the white rectangles slowly filling with green water. She flung the notebook in last; the small splash startled a blackbird on the far side of the pond which flew up from the thick grass, sunlight glistening on its wings.

She smiled at this sudden burst of surprised life, then, turning, sloshed slowly out of the pond. Without looking back, looking only at the house where she would begin her new life, she made her way through the deep and dewy grass.

18

BALLOWE:	Have you ever heard, Jaster, of the Prime Directive?
JASTER:	What do you—she must have done it! What is this—some kind of miserable trick?
BALLOWE:	Tell us about the Prime Directive, Jaster. Tell us now. It might help you later.
JASTER:	But this is ridiculous! I was summoned here to get an award for my work and now—

BALLOWE:	Let me ask you a question, Jaster, if you can manage to hold your tongue for one short moment: Why do you think we demons have been so successful in the last few hundred years—have you any idea? A guess perhaps? I'll tell you—the Prime Directive: The Doctrine of Nonexistence—our Master's greatest strategy. Wouldn't you agree that our greatest victory was to convince our subjects that we don't exist? Do you know the first dictum of the Doctrine?
JASTER:	Of course. Of course I do—but what is—
BALLOWE:	I'm waiting, Jaster, and I won't wait much longer.
JASTER:	Let Them Sleep. Every demon—
BALLOWE:	Well, well, so you *do* know. And what does that mean?
JASTER:	This is ridiculous. Absolutely absurd. I—am I to get an award or . . . or am I . . . No . . .
BALLOWE:	I'll tell you what it means: Keep their minds empty, prevent them from

waking up to life's possibilities, keep them stuffed with food, with money, let them worry about their little vanities, never alert them to our watchful presence, keep them from thinking of good and evil, disconnect them from their deepest impulses, substitute comfort for self-knowledge, smooth the way, so that they come to us yawning, their bellies full.

That's what your predecessor, Demon Torsk, did. He kept this girl from feeling even in the midst of upheaval. Even in the middle of a divorce she was complacent until you got hold of her. Satisfied with her life, small and circumscribed though it was. Until you got hold of her. We've been watching you for a long time, Jaster, for years actually, waiting for you to hang yourself.

And the subtraction strategy, the only thing you did that was halfway reasonable, was Torsk's idea—not yours, Jaster, not yours at all!

JASTER: Wh-what? Who told you that?

148
≈

BALLOWE: Admit it, Jaster. You read Torsk's notes on the case, then tried to pass off Torsk's strategy as your own. Of course there's nothing wrong with stealing in and of itself, but to have stolen an idea that he rejected as unworkable—it's exceedingly comic. Well? Isn't it? Do you deny it? I have his notes right here in front of me. I have to laugh, Jaster. Really, I must. What a ridiculous clown you are!

JASTER: I *absolutely* deny it! The subtraction strategy was *my* idea!

BALLOWE: Before you began your meddling, she belonged to us, she was firmly in our camp. Torsk knew that. That was why he ultimately rejected the subtraction strategy. He was afraid it might sensitize her to her loss, which, as we've proved here, it eventually did. He wrote in his notes: "Subtraction strategy is interesting, but could be dangerous." But you, you stupid fool, you couldn't resist, could you? You sensitized her to what she had lost, forced her to feel when her natural inclination

149
≈

was to deny feeling, to go dutifully along without a fuss. You should have left her alone to stew in her juices. But you couldn't, could you? After subtraction, you got her thinking of perfection. You got her thinking about Heaven and suffering and rebirth—of all the idiotic things! Until you came on the scene, we had her just where we wanted her, on the long, soft, pleasant path to Hell.

JASTER: I got her to hope! False hopes! Doomed hopes. Which will drive her to suicide! Which, after all, is the reason you called—

BALLOWE: Quiet, Jaster—you're going to make me start laughing again. Then came that business with the squirrel—she had no conception of death before that. No conception of mercy. She was perfectly happy in her little numerical world. Until you came along and dragged her out!

At this very moment, as we speak, she is talking to her mother in the

150
≈

kitchen. She is talking to her mother about good and evil, about life and death, love and hate. At dawn, as a gesture of defiance, she threw her notebook into the pond. The girl was not intent on drowning herself as you assumed, but on rebirth. All your talk about life and death loosed some deep, healing stream inside her.

JASTER: Remove this imbecile from my sight. I demand my rights! I demand that I be allowed to go back and—give me one more day with her. I have her right where I want her! You're too stupid to see that, of course. This is just a temporary setback—

BALLOWE: By the way, Jaster. For your own information, you would have been punished even if the girl had killed herself. We do not tolerate disobedience in any way, shape, or form. We would have welcomed a newcomer—suicides are always welcome—our Master would have been pleased. But not pleased at all by your unorthodox method.

Remove him! Bring him back in three months for sentencing.

Gentledemons—are we ready for our next candidate? Good. Guard—bring in the next one.

19

MEMORANDUM

TO: Ballowe, Chairman, Disciplinary Review

FROM: Lucifer, Secretary to His Most
Malign Magnificence

RE: Final Judgement on Demon 6166
(Demon Jaster)

Having reviewed the transcripts in the case of Demon 6166 (Demon Jaster); having had the usual three months to study the matter; and having reflected upon the damage Demon 6166's aberrant temptation has done to our just and glorious cause, we have concluded that the punishment in this case, as with all such cases, must be extremely severe.

Sources inform us that Demon 6166's tactics have most certainly alerted the girl to our presence. She is, because of these tactics, aware of both the beauty and the evil that flows through every day and every hour of her existence. She is alive to her capacities for both passivity and self-deception.

Demon Torsk, her former operative, reassigned to the case two months ago as a stop-gap measure, can't do a thing with her. She and her mother have reconciled. They talk openly to one another. They listen to each other. She and her father, always close, have grown even closer. They exchange letters at least twice a week. Love is growing up among them once more.

Torsk says it is doubtful we will ever have further success with her. Demon Jaster, with his meddling, has given her the wisdom of the serpent.

Therefore:

Effective immediately, 6166 (Demon Jaster) is to be demoted from Grade 10, Field Operative, to Grade 0, Fire Stoker Level 7. This will be a permanent reassignment.

May the Master have no mercy whatsoever on his soul.

About the Author

PETER SILSBEE is the versatile author of two highly praised books for young teens. *School Library Journal* called his first, *The Big Way Out,* "a strong story with fast action," adding that "the characters are well drawn, and evoke sympathy and concern." Of his humorous mystery-comedy cum romance, *Love Among the Hiccups, School Library Journal* said the "style is flawlessly consistent throughout. . . . The pace at which the mystery unfolds is quick and even, leading to a resolution with an unforeseen twist."

Peter Silsbee lists C. S. Lewis's *The Screwtape Letters* and Robertson Davies's *What's Bred in the Bone* among his favorite books.

The author, who has been a rock musician, a teacher, a publicist, and a research analyst, lives with his wife, Dede, in Brooklyn, New York.